# Casebook of
# The Voice

by

## Erwin K. Roberts
**based on the Voice's own recounting**

"Voice of Pain" originally appeared in *Double Danger Tales*
"Grand Opening: Under Fire" appeared in *Mystery Forum Magazine*
      and in *Double Danger Tales*
"Crime of the Arts" parts 1 thru 3 appeared in *Masked Gun Mystery*
      part 4 appears here for the first time.


Thanks to Tommy Hancock, Wayne Rangel & Shelby Vick for providing their photos for use in building this book's cover. Cover created using NewTek's Lightwave 3D software.

Printed in the United States of America


ISBN-13: 978-0615997414

Modern Knights Press
8505 E. 95th Terr
Kansas City, MO 64134

# Contents

As the stories above unfold,
the city's new FBI Agent-In-Charge
learns some of the history of the Voice.

**Metro Police Chiefs' Association Meeting & Christmas Party, December 1999**

The Dockery House they called it. Built by a timber baron who, so the story went, cut down every tree in Arkansas to make his fortune. Once where the nouveau rich butted heads with the east coast upper crust, the huge three story mansion served now as the region's history museum.

FBI Agent-In-Charge Reynolds parked his car in the employee's lot as instructed. His ID drew a wink from the older guy working the gate. Probably retired a L.E.O. (Law Enforcement Officer) of some kind, he mused. Reynolds looked around as he got out of the car and stretched. Under more than six inches of recent snow, only a couple of rabbit or squirrel tracks marred the smoothness of the rolling yards.

No snow remained on the lot or the sidewalk leading to the impressive three story stone structure. Built in the 1880's he recalled. The place managed to avoid the sometimes freakish pseudo-European looks that so many American buildings of the time affected. He decided he liked the place.

I'm the new kid on the block, he told himself. Here's where I learn the secret local handshake. Not to mention where some of the bodies are buried. Wish I'd been at the last meeting he sighed. Then maybe I would not have felt so helpless when we rolled into that kidnapping crime scene.

He headed up the wide stone stairs to the massive double doors remembering what he'd found.

# Voice of Pain

*Sometimes I wonder if it matters. Do I make a difference? All these years and the bad guys are still out there. Yeah, the stats are down... but a lot of the vermin are worse than ever. Even when I find them, I can't always stop them… in time.*

Police LT Ralph Adams pulled the microphone close to his mouth. "Tac One to control."

"Control center. Go."

Adams sighed and took a deep breath. "We're on scene. The area is secure. This is the right place. Suggest we go to Sierra Lima."

"Control, Sierra Lima authorized. Out"

Adams opened a case in the command van. He quickly activated the phone, called headquarters, and waited for scrambler to kick in. "Captain Rodriguez here, Adams. The Chief is with me. Go ahead."

"Who else is listening?"

"Just the two of us and the regular radio watch. None of the family involved, if that's what you're asking."

Adams relaxed, but only a tiny bit. "We have a bad situation. Identification is pending, but it's almost certain the girl is dead."

"How certain?"

"Major surprise if it isn't Grace Marten. It appears she has been dead for some time. They weren't planning to release her after the ransom was paid." Lights streamed across the van's windshield. "Looks like the FBI just rolled in. Now it'll hit the fan."

"Adams, this is the Chief. We half expected this outcome. What is the extra problem?"

Adams took a deep breath, closing his eyes as he continued, "The Voice beat us here."

*I drove the Imagemaker away from that place. I seethed with emotions. Rage fought with despair. Exhaustion both mental and physical added to the tears that ran down my mask. You can't win them all. I knew that. You can't win them all. But a six year old girl. I couldn't have saved her even if I had been quicker. Maybe she'd died by accident, but probably they just killed her to keep things simpler. She'd been dead for hours, several…*

The silence over the Sierra Lima (Secure Line) ended. Rodriguez asked, "You're sure about the Voice?"

"Dead sure," replied Adams. "His marks are all over the place. Some of the perps are asleep. Lookouts, probably. He got in quietly, I'm guessing. Then he found the girl. After that he took the gloves off. Everyone else is dead, including Richardson, one of our suspects for inside man. I've seen at least two of the Voice's fancy throwing knives sticking out of people. The rest are a combination of firepower and hand to hand."

*I finally pulled the van over to strip off the door and side decals.*

*As I changed the plates I wondered, what now? No loose ends of this case. I clearly remembered the inside man heading for the front door while clawing for a weapon. The 40 MM round of double ought buckshot sent him outside without opening the door.*

"What am I supposed to tell the FBI?" asked Adams.

Silence, for the count of three. Then the Chief said, "Who's talking to them?"

"Reece, the SWAT team leader. We decided to show them the body first. It might keep them more focused on the victim, than asking about the Voice. I wish Agent Morgan hadn't retired. Does this new AIC Reynolds know anything about the Voice?"

Rodriguez responded. "If Morgan told him anything I haven't heard. We walked on eggshells around Reynolds at Headquarters today. We knew if the Voice was in town he'd take an hand."

"I called Morgan," began the Chief. "He was a bit coy about it. Said he referred Reynolds to some FBI archives about similar folks. He also told me he didn't know Reynolds well enough to guess how he'd react to an Independent Operator."

*What to do now. There are a dozen major drug dealers in town I can take my anger out on with absolutely no regrets. But what good will that do me? Can't just drive around till I'm exhausted and hope I don't have nightmares when I finally sleep. Can't... no, don't want to call Doc Wanamaker. He'll insist I spend a bunch of time at his guest ranch for the rich, famous, and flustered.*

Agent-In-Charge Jeffrey Reynolds looked at the carnage, then back at the small body. He wasn't sure just what he had expected, but it sure wasn't this.

He'd come to this mid-western town from San Francisco where there were more eccentrics per square foot than maybe any city on the planet. He'd heard that the cops in this metro were good. Nothing in the three months he'd been here contradicted that. But there was something different about this town. Everyone he got introduced to in government, and even the media, seemed to be overly interested in what he thought of the town. They all seemed to have this "I wonder if I know something you don't." look about them.

Even Morgan, the man he'd replaced, seemed a little ill at ease discussing the local situation. Morgan hesitated talking about some things, while he readily spoke on other subjects, like certain informants who were guaranteed to be OK. Then, on his last trip to headquarters Morgan had insisted he see, even made him an appointment, to go through the classified Non-Traditional Operations archive. That turned out to be even further back in the cellar than those infamous UFO chasers.

Now, only now, a little light showed through the mental haze.

*A light blinked at me when I opened the door to one of my semi-public apartments. It wasn't one of several alarms. It simply blinked on the answering machine connected to a phone whose number usually couldn't be found, even by tele-marketers. I ignored it.*

*I locked the door, including the secret sliding bars that made the door three times harder to break than going through the walls. This building rose five floors above its neighbors and on my southern side no one could look in my windows without a helicopter, or repelling gear.*

*I pivoted the entertainment center outward to reveal a lighted makeup table. I sat down and just stared at myself for a minute. Then my fingers couldn't move fast enough to tear off my mask. I grabbed the solvents needed to remove the base coat of makeup. Done with the removal, I headed for the shower leaving a trail of clothing, weapons, and emotions.*

Agent-In-Charge Reynolds sat in the Command Van facing Adams who offered him coffee and wondered what direction the Fed's first question would take.

"Adams, I'm not going to hassle about basic jurisdiction. We were within minutes of the deadline. Your people passed the intel to us quickly. You were much closer with a highly trained team, so you went in. Its also obvious that, right or wrong choice to go in, you could not have saved Grace. Any discussion on that issue can wait.

"I need to know what happened here. Your people are pussyfooting around me like I'm a bomb that needs defusing. Most of the perps are dead, but your officers don't seem concerned. Well, maybe that isn't exactly the right term. Your team leader says this is the way you found the scene. And he didn't seem all that surprised about it.

"I know I'm new to this town, but if I don't get some answers I might come to the wrong conclusions about what your people did, or didn't do."

Adams stopped holding his mental breath as he handed over the cup of coffee. "I'm to give you the short version," he began. "The Chief will be happy to talk to you after he notifies the family. To start with, did you notice the knives?"

"I didn't have time for a very close look," remarked Reynolds, "but they looked like custom throwing knives."

"That's right, very custom. If you know where to look, you'll find what amounts to serial numbers on them. I assume you saw that the two living suspects were drugged…"

"Sure. Seemed at odds with the others being dead."

"Agent Reynolds, like you said, you're new to this town. Not me. I'm third generation Cop. When I was growing up, even before I was supposed to listen, I heard my dad and two of my uncles talking about criminals found asleep in the places they were robbing. Of violent crimes being broken up by knives just like those, only not thrown to kill, mostly. Well those stories were still going around when I joined the force. And stories about someone who could look and sound like anyone. And stories about a source who spoke with an inhuman sound that no one could imitate. Sounds like a campfire tale, doesn't it?"

"I'd ask what you were smoking around that campfire," said Reynolds, "except for one thing. AIC Morgan twisted my arm into spending a whole morning reading classified official reports about men and a few women who did just the sort of things you're describing. If you repeat this, I'll deny I ever said it, but some of them actually worked for the Bureau back when. The most recent report I saw was dated in the late sixties. Concerned a disguise artist referred to as 'Mr. Jones.'"

"Well, Agent Reynolds, tonight you have seen the aftermath of the man we refer to as 'The Voice.'"

"This is his typical work?" asked Reynolds feeling a mixture of astonishment and outrage. "Don't tell me this whole metro area, press included, tolerates a *Death Wish* style killer."

Surprised that the outburst hadn't been more explosive, Adams took a sip of the van's mud based coffee. "This is very atypical of the Voice's work. The Chief may have better figures, but by my estimates, eighty-five per cent of the time no one knows that they're dealing with him. He's a source on the other end of a phone line. He must have dozens of identities. He calls a cop, a prosecutor, a reporter. He gives information. He may have been the cop's source for fifteen years. Maybe you've seen this source in person, maybe not, but you don't know it's the Voice.

"Fourteen more per cent of the time the phone rings and you hear *the Voice*! A voice our best audio techs can't begin to explain. I hope the Chief plays you a recording, 'cause words… well they just aren't enough.

"When you hear *the Voice* you know the situation is urgent. Something major is going to land in your lap. And you had better believe him. History has shown that major bad guys get away, or civilians suffer if you ignore him. If he says something might happen, it almost always does. He says something probably will happen… well, he might as well be saying the sun's going to come up in the morning.

"Tonight is the other one per cent, maybe even less than one per cent. When lives are on the line and time is short he goes in. He uses a very potent knockout gas when he can. You saw the two sleeping beauties. Reece probably told you we figure them for lookouts. He found the girl. Then he went hunting. Probably had the gas gun in one hand and a throwing knife the other. Once they started shooting he put the gas gun away and pulled out some high rate of fire room broom. He ran out of knives he used a small grenade launcher he sometimes carries."

"The door," breathed Reynolds.

"The door," repeated Adams. "The weapon appears to be a cut down version of the Army's old breach loader from the early Viet Nam era. He seems to have a few home brewed rounds for the thing. This time though, he used the standard shotgun round. I don't remember how many pellets can fit in 40 millimeters, but it's a bunch. At least four of the pellets hit the gun Richardson was trying to yank out of his belt. Folded him up and sent him through the door. We don't see this very often. What comes next is the big question."

*What next? What do I do for an encore? I'm exhausted. Mentally exhausted. Physically exhausted. I'd love to go roust some big time drug merchants. I'm too tired and I don't need or want the other problems taking a stimulant will cause. I want to work this mad off, but I'm too damned tired.*

*I finally came out of the bathroom. I must have come close to emptying the hot water tank. I was clean and totally depressed. New lights blinked at me. Three of the four cell phones on the makeup table demanded attention. One would be from Doc. The other two, I didn't really need to check. George Sanchez would be one. My Burbank. The other would be her. Those same lights would be blinking in my other places on specially cloned cell phones. A light also blinked on the building intercom. The intercom taken out of service many years ago.*

"Next from whom? Him? The Media?" AIC Reynolds wondered if his feet were anywhere near the bottom of the swamp he felt himself sinking into.

"Him. The guy must be able to bottle up his emotions like some Yogi, or something. He seems to live undercover almost all the time. The few times something like tonight goes down, especially with a tragic ending, we get one of two follow-ups. Sometimes he leaves town for a while. Sources believed to be him vanish. If someone's expecting a call, it gets canceled. That's the easy part.

"On the other hand, when he's got a real mad to work off, strange things happen. No one knows why, but he's especially got it in for drug wholesalers. At times like this big shots' stately homes develop gas leaks, become infested with hornets, other fun stuff. Their pleasure boats sink. And that's just what we know about.

"My favorite story, can't help laughing, nobody had a clue this upstanding guy was into drugs. You know those big seeding machines? You put grass seed in a small hopper and bales of hay in a huge one? I rolled backup on this unknown trouble call. We found one of these monster machines parked next to this bum's front wall. The thing was chugging away, seeding the yard. Was empty by the time we got it turned off. Over one thousand pounds of high quality Pot landed in that yard, seeds and all. His own stock, as it turned out. DEA took the hint and started digging. The bozo's in prison, and the new owner of the property has just about got the hemp to stop sprouting every spring."

"You mean he doesn't just shoot them?"

"No, not so far as we can tell. I'm sure the Chief is expecting some Silly Stuff calls tonight or tomorrow. Let's hope he just drops out of sight for a while."

*Count your blessings, the song says. Fall asleep counting your blessings. Well, the only blessing I saw worthy of the title had to be that someone else had to tell the family that not the police, the Feds, not even some Wil Of the Wisp had been quick enough to find the girl alive. Try sleeping on that sole blessing. Try not having nightmares. What if I'd leaned on that reluctant source first. But I'd polled some wise guys whose dark sides didn't extend to crimes against children. Some even seemed sorry they couldn't help. Would that have saved enough time? I turned back to the door as the intercom buzzed.*

"Reynolds, this incident with the Voice happened just before we could bring you into the loop," began the Chief. "Our meeting's set in about two weeks."

"Sounds like you've started a fan club," snorted Reynolds.

"No not really. I'm talking about our local Police Chief's Association. You've been in and out of town so much you missed two meetings. You should have your invitation to the next one in a day or two. Its mostly local business, but you and the senior Marshall, Secret Service, and military CID are always welcome. Some meetings are more social than business. For your first meeting the entire agenda would have been the Voice."

*Short of stalking back out on the streets, I knew I was beaten. Doc would have a field day if I told him I came here without thinking. I have several places where I am the landlord and no one notices my comings and goings. But this is her building. She follows the news. She would know I'd be in the chase up to my neck. She'd keep an eye out for any of my usual faces to come in. She'll be knocking on the front door next. I gave in and pressed the button on the intercom.*

"You know Reynolds, I retire in a year or two. When I was a rookie stories about the Voice were just beginning. Nobody took much stock in them. Then things started to happened that mattered. Especially on the corruption front. Things were fairly wide open. Not that much showed on the surface. But there was always someone who knew somebody that could get your problem fixed for enough money, or other considerations. The local media didn't want to make waves. Might hurt the bottom line.

"Somebody, probably the Voice, would drop a dime on someone with a little protection. Nothing happened. So he changed tactics. Network news directors would get bundles of documentation on payoffs and drug deals. Then they'd want to know why the local affiliate wasn't covering a major story. Local media owners started getting a midnight visitor who showed them the score and demanded action. Feds like you got tips that put them on scene of crimes that local forces should have handled. The State Attorney General got those same visits.

"As far as I know one of my predecessors became the first local cop to meet the Voice face to face. Happened one night when his wife and kids were out of town. He woke up to find someone in his bedroom. Sitting in the bedside chair was this figure in bulky, shape hiding coveralls. Had this shroud like mask over his head. I've seen similar things advertised in trade mags as a 'sniper's veil.'

"The Chief told me he nearly got cross-eyed looking down the weird pistol pointing at him. Being an old OSS man, he'd seen all kinds of special weapons. This one he didn't recognize. He decided to think of his visitor as The Vail. That is until he spoke. If the Chief Hadn't dubbed him The Voice, someone else would have."

*That always smooth alto rolled out of the speaker. "I wondered how long I'd have to wait. You could have called me, you know."*

*"I didn't want to bother you," I said. I didn't sound very convincing, even to myself.*

*"That's most of your troubles," she said a little impatiently. "Too much the lone wolf." She paused waiting for my reaction. "Now come on up." When I failed to answer she continued, "Don't play quiet games with me. If I have to wake my other tenants by pounding on your door with a hammer I will."*

*"Let me finish dressing," I replied, trying to remember if I had any quick apply masks in the apartment.*

*"By the way, its two thirty in the morning. I've turned off the elevator. No one will probably notice. But if you do have the energy to go down all those stairs, you'll set off the alarm when you leave..."*

*"I'll be up in five minutes," I said. She'd won.*

The Chief faded down the recorder. Reynolds checked to see if his mouth hung open. Never in his life had he heard speech like that. Clearly understandable, but it changed constantly. Tone, octave, pitch, varied with total randomness. Speed and any strong inflection appeared more under control. He noticed the Chief watching out of the corner of his eye, waiting. Finally he took a deep breath.

"You're reaction is about typical, Reynolds. I've heard that voice called a lot of things: from the Twilight Zone, Linda Blair on steroids, cursed, unholy, and more. We relayed that particular call to the S.E.C. about six weeks ago. Got them to pull out all the stops, and quick. Kept the CEO and Chief Financial Officer of the corporation from sending about seventy-five million dollars offshore. Because of the Voice those two will probably do time and the reorganization of the company will save over six hundred jobs locally. That is the usual way we knowingly deal with the Voice. He's simply the best source possible.

"Anyway, my predecessor, Cobbins, heard that voice cold one night. The Voice told Cobbins chapter and verse about corruption on the force, and at the County and State levels. He left behind the first of what became known as Snare Packages. Names, dates, account numbers, hidden safes, pictures, you name it. Everything needed to trip up a crook. The next week Cobbins put together a special detail he knew he could trust and got to work. Intel kept showing up. Before the year ended State and Federal Indictments came through. And from the top, down, mostly.

"With his help we've managed to stay pretty clean. Several times promising Officers have resigned with no notice or apparent reason. A few days later I'll get a Snare Package. Usually there's not enough to be actionable, but I end up mighty glad the man or woman is not going to drag the force down with them.

"Now about tonight… I suggest you file a preliminary report of how 'acting on information received' you went to the scene and found so-and-so. More information to follow. Then come to the Chiefs Association meeting. I'll see if I can move up the date. Morgan will be there, too. (Though I figure you'll want to debrief him before hand.) At the meeting you'll even learn why the Secret Service sometimes asks for his help. Now about the press waiting outside…"

Reynolds decided that the swamp he'd been treading water in for the past few hours might actually be shallow enough to stand. Now he knew why the Deputy Director called his new assignment "interesting." He also stopped wondering why he'd been selected for this position over a couple of competent, but hidebound, by-the-bookers. He decided that when the dust settled a bit he'd drive up to see his Great Uncle Lynn. Ask him about Non-Traditional Operations back in the wild old days.

*I threw on slacks and a t-shirt, secured the weapons and pushed the entertainment center back in place. Back in the bathroom I opened a section of wall tile and stepped onto a ladder in a utility shaft. I climbed.*

*When she bought this building I helped her put in a few specials. She lives two floors above my recluse's lair. She keeps two small guest apartments on the floor between. Cleverly carved from that space is a tiny efficiency that can only be reached from above or below.*

*As I stepped through the panel into the closet I saw the light coming under the door dim. She'd used her entrance behind the Murphy Ironing Board in the kitchenette and beat me. Well, maybe she'd even used the intercom from here.*

*Some media reviewer once said, "The more expensive the meal, the darker the venue." Think of the third most expensive meal you've ever had. That's how much light remained.*

I closed the closet door and stood about two feet in front of her. She greeted me as she always does. She put her hands to my forehead and ran them slowly down the sides of my face. Aside from Doc, she is the only person who touches my true face.

I returned the gesture and felt skin much smoother than the last time. I must have paused ever so briefly, for she said, "Four more small procedures. The manager of the shelter and my secretary know what I really look like now."

"That's a big change," I began.

"Yes it is, but we're not going to discuss that. We're going to discuss you! You're exhausted. I can hear it. I could feel it. You should be asleep. How long have you been up this time? Two days? Four days."

"Only about thirty hours," I said, "and no pills!"

"Well, thank God for small favors. I still get chills thinking what just one of Doc Wanamaker's Wakers did to me that time. Now let's get you some rest."

"But I can't go to sleep..."

"Not can't, don't want to. You're afraid of the nightmares. Your mind can accept failure." She put her hands on my chest. "But your heart can't. I'm probably the best example of how you don't allow failure.

"When you saved me from that rich kid serial killer my face was in shreds, and my mind was even worse off. You held me together. Got me expert treatment when you could have dumped me at any emergency room. I looked like I'd been in a meat grinder. I was a mental basket case and you knew I was street trash."

"You weren't street trash," I began. Her hand quickly covered my mouth. As she spoke I felt her pulse quicken even though she never raised her voice.

"Street trash! If that psycho hadn't picked me I'd be dead today. Bad drugs or AIDS. I popped pills like crazy. I did whatever it took to get more. That's street trash. But you still rode to my rescue like an urban knight. Saved me. Flimflammed the whole world so I inherited that scum's money. Saw that Doc Wanamaker gave me the royal treatment both physical and mental.

"I'll bet the old boy never even told you I tried to kill myself. Four times. I didn't care. My life was over. Know how he stopped me? He told me if I succeeded, I'd hurt you. He told me about the times he'd stitched you up, set your bones. Said he could fix most physical things, but he couldn't do much if you lost your mental edge. Before that I'd done a lot of brooding and screaming, but I'd never cried. Until then. That's when I *decided to get well. With a lot of help from Doc and others I did. Sort of.*

*"As an outpatient I existed in a dark apartment zoning out on bad TV. I never looked all that great, but then I could barely let the medical professionals look at my face. That's not living. Then you showed up and rescued me again. You taught me some of your makeup. I wasn't my own jailer anymore.*

*"Now I have a life. Not a conventional one, but a good one. I started spending the slime's money by founding the Battered Persons Shelter. I went to school. You've even let me help you in small ways. But you never let me help you in big ways."*

*Her hand dropped from my mouth, slid along my chest, then down to my hand. She drew me across the room. With the other hand she turned down the bed.*

*"Kick your shoes off and get in," she told me. I was far too tired to argue. While I lay down she moved a high backed chair against the bed, facing the head. "You think I spent all those nights getting a PhD in Psychology just to help out at the shelter? I've been trying to figure myself out, and you, especially you, for the past ten years. Maybe I can't stop the nightmares. But if they come, I'll be here to wake you."*

*I looked up at her shadowy figure. Touched her hand and closed my eyes.*

## Metro Police Chiefs' Association Meeting

"Welcome, Agent Reynolds," said an erect old man as he entered the museum building. "I'm Jerome Cobbins. Aside from being a long retired Chief of Police, I'm on the museum board. That makes me host for tonight's get together."

Reynolds decided Cobbins had never been a physically large man. But his presence still seemed strong for a World War Two veteran this close to the end of the twentieth century. Twenty or thirty years ago he probably could stare down a bear, or a perp, just like Davy Crockett.

"I've heard a thing or two about you Chief. I'll be glad of your input on tonight's special topic," Reynolds remarked in an easy voice.

Cobbins grinned. "Right to the point. I like that. Reason I met you here is for a heads up. You're not the only one who's going to learn about the Voice tonight. We've got the three out of town candidates for the Poplar Park job here tonight. They think its strictly social. If you like, you can sit and pretend its all old news to you. Your call. The rest of us will play along. No need to answer now. We've got an excellent dinner before all that starts."

Reynolds pondered as Cobbins lead him up a marble staircase. "Did you often have direct contact with the Voice?"

"Not hardly. Got to be a standing joke for those in the know. I'd be out of town on business, or even vacation when he'd pop up. Or in the hospital throwing a kidney stone or two. About 1977 there was a bank job…"

## GRAND OPENING… UNDER FIRE

A new branch bank. Free yardsticks and punch. (What more could you want in 1977, an adding machine?) Bring money! Take home a banana plant.

I don't have a regular home these days. My potted plants usually die. I have no conceivable use for a yardstick. However, I deal frequently with money. That's why I went in just before closing. Better get to know these people. They might be helpful when I need some exotic financial service in a hurry.

I stopped at one of my apartments to change my face. Placing the old one in a jar of conditioner, I began by touching up my makeup base coat. That done, I slipped in the cheek spreader and added an appliance to the bridge of my nose. The face mask came next, I re-combed my hair, did touch-ups, and slipped into another outfit. Total time: two minutes and fifty-three seconds. I hadn't been in a hurry.

Hiding the Colt Commander, I rummaged in the weapons locker. I selected a tear-gas pen, a garrote for inside my tie, a pocket knife, and a Cobra electro-shock cigar case. Since this was a social trip, I left the heavy stuff behind.

As Jim Norris, the apartment's tenant, I departed while still adjusting the device in my throat to reach his deep bass voice range.

It was a bank all right. Like most, done in contemporary boring and potted palms. The branch manager had been shaking hands so long I'll bet he wanted to get potted himself. The punch tasted surprisingly good. I opened both savings and checking accounts with enough to rate everything on the free list. I arranged for the booty to go to a neighborhood church. This entitled me to a personal introduction to the manager.

While waiting to speak to him, I surveyed the small crowd of customers. I noticed two little old ladies. Beyond them stood a junior exec type and a teen in a fast food uniform. Two tellers faced them. At the loan desk sat a man in coveralls and a teen in a wheel chair.

A guard glanced at his watch. It was three minutes until closing. Two men came in, one with lots of red hair and large fluffy sideburns. The second had a bald head that gleamed behind huge sunglasses. A sling, white against his brown jacket, completely hid one arm. As the two passed me I smelled spirit gum. Makeup? Why? Before I could move, the manager wrung my hand. Five seconds later another pair in stocking masks with sawed off shotguns rushed in.

I took a deep breath. Then I glanced after the first two. Red-and-fuzzy slipped a Saturday Night Special out of his belt. Everybody in the bank stood in a cross-fire. The two shotgunners moved in front of large plants, invisible from the street.

"No one move! Hands up! You employees, back away from your places. No alarms! Red, get the bags," spat the left hand shotgunner with the green jacket.

I looked back at Red. He pulled paper bags and a roll of masking tape out of a jacket pocket and headed for the security cameras. Then I saw what Kojak with the brown jacket had covered with his sling: a wire stocked Uzi sub-machine gun. I swore silently. Dad told me there'd be days like this.

Red finished with the cameras, then disarmed the two guards. One at a time he frisked us. He took my pocket knife. I hoped he'd cut himself. One blade is poisoned.

We were herded into a corner. Red and the other gunner (blue jacket) cleaned out the tills.

"Not as much as we figured," grunted Blue. "Come on manager, open the vault." With the vault finished, he confronted the manager in a disgusted tome. "Still not much, how come?"

"Well, ahh…" sputtered the manager, "Most all of our larger depositors use checks or other instruments. Its s-safer, you know…"

Blue seemed about to hit the poor guy, but said, "Show me the Traveler's Checks and Money Orders."

That's when the police arrived.

The warning came on a walkie-talkie hidden under the green coat. "Pigs! Pigs! Two cars at each end of the street. Moving in from both sides." Added were several common four-letter words from all.

A moment later Blue assessed the situation. "We're stuck. Too many to shoot our way out. It'll take a full SWAT assault to get us. We'll try to bargain. Red, take the hostages into the lounge. You people don't try anything stupid, or you'll die."

We were quickly moved into the employee break area. I helped to get the wheelchair through the narrow door, then huddled with the others against the far wall while Red ripped out the phone cord. He moved to the door and told us to sit down.

If this turned into of those *Dog Day Afternoon* protracted media events, I would be in trouble. In five hours, or so, the base coat of my makeup had to be removed. If I didn't get it off my face would become inflamed, then infected. My mask would become obvious, after which everything would hit the fan. I harbored no doubts that whoever these yo-yo's turned out to be, they'd kill easy and often to stay free. I decided that Jim Norris would probably be lost to me.

I reached into my jacket. "Stop!" snapped Red.

I gave him an innocent startled look. "I - I need a smoke, bad," I said, whispering a small prayer that no one here was enough of a non-smoker to object. "Look, you saw the case. Please let me get it out."

When he didn't complain, I pulled the case out with two fingers. While looking very innocent, that grip actually brought the electrical weapon to full charge. Originally designed by Alf Levine as a stun shocker with foot-long probes, mine has a fail-safe circuit that discharges the Cobra's total energy into the next thing to touch it.

Slowly, I removed a thin cigar. I put it in my mouth saying, "Here, have one.." I was obviously too far away to hand him the case, or to jump him. I threw the case.

The Cobra cut a high arc. Red instinctively reached upward. His gun pointed way over our heads as he caught the case. And jerked.

There was a snap. Everyone's hair stood up. Red fell. I caught him and removed the gun from his limp fingers.

I took stock as I locked the door. When the others began to fidget, I shushed them. I crammed a chair under the doorknob. Red's .32 caliber toy held six. I found six more shells racked in a quick loader, plus my knife. That Hong Kong pea-shooter'd be small help at ranges over ten feet. No other way out, except possibly the dropped ceiling.

"Can anyone fix the phone," I asked without much hope?

"Sure!" said the kid in the wheelchair. "Its only four wires. But you make a call and I'll bet other phones light up outside here. I can see the main box down under that table. That'll be better." He flipped open one armrest to produce a small tool kit. "Dad, help me."

I got the others under what cover there was. Their nerves were shaken, but they obeyed the forceful tone I used. Finished, I found the kid propped against the wall. His father braced him and held the tools, The side of his wheelchair sported a bumper sticker that read "Yo Soy Chicano."

I pulled the table further out of his way. "Como se llama, amigo?" I asked in my so-so Spanish. He had pity on me and replied in English.

"I'm George Sanchez. How much current did that thing deliver?"

"Too much," I said. "He's barely alive. Can you handle the spaghetti?"

"Sure, electronics is my hobby. I'm hooking into the repairman's terminal. In a minute you can dial out safely and, with this extra wire I cut off the ripped up phone, I can tap any phone in the building. What do you need?"

What a break. Here someone had a useful skill and didn't need a nerve tonic. "That outside line, please."

George handed me the instrument. I punched a familiar number and turned away. One quick adjustment put my voice to the outer limits. The device, designed by an old Chinese mimic and a battlefield surgeon worked its magic. My voice became unique.

"Major Case Squad, Carpenter." replied a voice that I knew very well.

"Listen carefully," I said with out preamble. My voice rasped and grated. It sounded in general need of an exorcism. Carpenter grunted, but stayed quiet. "You know the Rudolph Bank job?"

"Sure, Forty-Second and Fenwick. Several hostages. You have something for us?"

"Yes, I'm one of the hostages." The earphone chuckled briefly. I glanced around the room. I could see that one of the security men might have heard about the Voice. "Four men inside. I've taken out one, and I'm barricaded in the employee's lounge with all other hostages. We're undiscovered, as yet. Two men with sawed-off shotguns. One with wire-stocked Uzi machine pistol. Possible hand weapons. A spotter with radio warned them when you moved in. Almost a paramilitary operation."

As I spoke, I stripped the sideburns and wig from Red. "I have a make on my prisoner. Sam Winston, a/k/a/ Tau Libra. This must be a T.P.F. fund raiser."

The air turned blue around the receiver.

Most of the other hostages got the message. I turned to silence their frightened mumbling.

T.P.F., The People's Front, claimed that corrupt society must pay for its own destruction at T.P.F. hands. They liberated wealth lots more often than they attacked social structures. They left very few witnesses.

Carpenter quit cursing. "Can you hold out during an assault?"

"No way," I whispered into the receiver. "Two loads of shot and we've got Dutch Doors. I'll have to pull them from here while you bust in. Who's in charge?"

He hesitated. "Chief Cobbins is out of town. The Deputy Chief's on the way. Until then Tim Kelly is in charge. Once the Deputy gets there, the talk will start. I've still got pain from the last time we 'talked' to that bunch. Wait two minutes and call 555-3742. For the record I'll tell Tim you're a deep cover Fed I know. Good luck, but don't expect my help so easy next time. I'll doctor this call's audio tape at 'Federal request...'"

As I waited, I locked eyes with the bank manager. "How'd you trip the alarm?" my graveyard voice demanded.

He winced at every word. "Th... They did it themselves. When more than two cameras lose signal, the alarm goes off automatically. New system."

"Hah! The People's Front gets taken by its own cleverness." I cut the rasping laugh, since it upset the others.

I punched numbers.

"Command Post, Sergeant Kelly."

"Did Carpenter call you?"

"Yes, and not even the name of your 'agency.' What gives?"

I recapped the situation, warning about the spotter. We threw a quick plan together. "That does it Sarge. I'll be wearing... Hey, you two, get that turkey's clothes off... gray slacks and a cream wind-breaker. I'm borrowing his red wig and sideburns."

While waiting for Kelly to pass the word I investigated the drop ceiling. The teen in the chicken uniform weighed over two hundred. I stood on his shoulders. The bank designers had thought of this trick. Heavy metal mesh extended above the walls and covered all the holes. I could see alarm leads attached. Scratch one bright idea.

Hopping down, I announced, "Got to do this the hard way. Everybody get as far to the side of the door as possible. Manager, as soon as I leave, have the men help you get everything that moves against the door. George, stay on the phone. Keep absolutely quiet, if you value your lives." I heard George Sanchez whisper into the phone as I slipped out the door.

I held my breath as I peeked out. I didn't look much like Sam Winston, but the wig and burns would buy time. I'd adjusted my voice, but Winston had spoken so little that I only had a rough approximation on him. Thank the Lord for favors, large and small. The corridor was empty.

Three quick, quiet steps and I reached the dead end. Empty, with no exit. I checked the rest rooms and a couple of offices. Also empty. Only one way to go, forward to the enemy's rear.

A recent design fad hates straight lines. The corridor dog-legged into the main open area. I hit the floor and scooted forward. For self-proclaimed elitist terrorists, they'd done some honest-looking work as movers. Everything that wasn't nailed down, and some that had been, formed a barricade.

Blue, Green, and Brown positioned themselves wide apart. With Red's Saturday-Night-Special I'd never get all three trigger-happy T.P.F.'s, or hold them until SWAT broke through. I backed down the corridor.

As planned, someone answered my special knock at the lounge. "Listen up. I'm going to fire one shot in the Ladies room across the hall. I want everybody to scream, then be super-quiet. Tell the police not to move until they hear more gunfire." I listened to a muffled acknowledgment.

I stepped quickly into the rest room. I plugged my ears the best I could and squeezed the trigger. The slug tore up through the paper towels in a full holder and disappeared into the ceiling. Back across the hall, the screaming lasted about three seconds. If my ears hadn't been ringing, I could have heard a fly walking.

The color kids probably expected a police rush with the shot. When none came, they decided to check on Red. Blue came back and rapped on the door from the side.

"Red, what the Hell happened? I guess the Pigs didn't hear-r-r..." My garrote whipped over his head. Even in the energy conserving dim light, rage and terror flashed across his face. I tightened the loop's built in ratchet to cut off his sound and air. I grabbed the shotgun just before he could get his finger back in the trigger guard. As his struggles weakened, I shoved him into the rest room, then headfirst into the wall. If the garrote wasn't too tight, he might live through this. Not that I really cared. He carried some shotgun shells, plus a shiny Luger and two spare magazines.

Knowing The People's Front, I didn't ask them to surrender. I looked around the corner, spotted Brown with his Uzi, aimed the shotgun and fired.

As his leaking body fell, I pumped another shell into position. I saw Green began to move when the plate glass window at the side of the barricade started sprouting holes, then it quickly cascaded to the floor. Three men in blue-black flack jackets dived in. I leaned against the wall and relaxed.

They spread out and took control with massive firepower while other officers poured in. I held the shotgun far from the trigger and didn't move.

Quickly I became the apex of multiple lines of fire. "Where's Kelly?" I asked, almost before someone bluntly requested that I drop the shotgun.

"The safety's off," I noted as I leaned the weapon against the wall. Before the subjects of handcuffs, or the position, could be discussed, I spotted Kelly climbing in.

"Sergeant Kelly, could you assist me over here?" We swapped prearranged passwords, and he quickly escorted me out to the street, just in time...

...for the big climax. As we got into the street, Kelly started to remind me about the big favor I owed him and Carpenter. A motor started behind us. I figured it as a SWAT vehicle. Suddenly the motor roared like a dragster. Tires screamed. Kelly and I spun around to see a UPS truck lurch toward us from the curb.

The spotter. It had to be. The truck had enough weight to crash the two sedan blockage at the corner.

I clawed out the Luger and the little .32.

I'm not sure how many rounds I fired before I dived across the hood of a parked Valiant. Getting to my feet, I heard the cops at the road block cut loose. Glancing across the street, I hoped not to see Kelly splattered on the ground.

To my surprise, he popped up from between two parked cars. From under his gear, somewhere, he pulled out a .44 Magnum hand cannon and started sending large chunks of metal after the UPS tuck.

Kelly, or somebody, hit something vital. The truck veered left and demolished a parked Cadillac, and a VW Bug.

Cops converged on the truck from all directions. That, I decided, had to be my cue. I slipped into the nearby H. Salt Fish and Chips place, and hurried out the back. I figured I'd just have time to clean out Jim Norris"s apartment before Kelly and his buddies arrived.

## Metro Police Chiefs' Association Meeting

"I landed coming back from a Washington conference less than an hour after the shootout," remarked Cobbins as they reached the top of the round staircase. "All the top news reporters and crews were still turning over every rock and manhole cover in that Fenwick neighborhood. I got met by a swarm of second stringers, news interns, and even one weather forecaster who happened to live near the airport. They wanted details of an event I did not even know existed. Probably felt about the same way you did last week, you think?"

Reynolds couldn't keep a snort of a laugh from escaping. "Blind sided, for sure, Chief. I never knew the so-called Independent Operators existed outside of pulp fiction."

"They pretty much faded away during the Cold War. Way too many paranoids at the Federal level in those days." Cobbins led the way through a roped off parlor towards the rear of the mansion. "During the War. World War Two, that is, some of them worked almost openly in the war effort. I met a couple of them on jobs for the O.S.S. They weren't completely an American deal, either. I even knew of one Aussie who served with their military while wearing a mask. Used the code name 'Phantom Commando.'"

Reynolds whistled. "That I'll have to put that into a search engine just to see what pops up!"

"Don't expect much," cautioned Cobbins. "Fellow name of Dixon started an Aussie comic book about him. Plus that's what the Germans called Arnold's movie *Commando*. I figure most links will lead there. Now, before we step into the dining room, I got a tip while I waited for you. Word is that one of the Poplar Park candidates has potential problems. Don't be surprised if things take a strange turn."

Cobbins opened the door. The sound of casual conversation drifted over them. The room held six round tables set with five places so as nobody had their backs totally to the raised stage at the front. Most of the seats were full of people in civilian clothes.

"This being the Christmas party," remarked Cobbins, "there are several more retirees like me than at most meetings. We've placed you at the center of the first row.

"Lady and gentlemen, this is FBI Agent-In-Charge Jeffrey Reynolds. This is the first meeting he's been able to make. Please introduce yourselves."

"Good evening, Agent Reynolds. I'm Sarah Mitchell, Deputy

Chief of the third largest city in New Hampshire. Like the other candidates I'm being interviewed tomorrow for the Poplar Park position."

"Hello again. We met very briefly at last month's symposium on the drug trade. I'm Major McTeal. Used to head up the Northwest Patrol until those oak leaves came through this summer. I'm also in the Poplar Park matrix."

"A man your size is hard to forget, Major. I also remember the Sheriff here. My boys and I spent a great weekend camping in your county's big park last month. But I don't know you, sir."

"No reason why you should, Agent Reynolds. I'm no longer a sworn officer. Name's Michael Christman. I just helped Sheriff Miller's department get some information off of an old Commodore Vic-20. Then he invited me here to plug my Computer Forensics consulting firm."

"So this is your first trip to this area?"

"Not hardly. Six years ago some of you Feds convinced me to go undercover here. 'Bout got me killed. But a certain Independent saved my bacon. You know who I mean?"

"I think I do," said Reynolds with a sigh.

Christman opened a briefcase to extract a thick envelope. "Then you might get a kick out of this. I'm shopping around this highly fictionalized screenplay of the case. You'll probably get a laugh or two out of it."

Reynolds leaned the envelope against his chair as the servers showed up for drink orders.

Salad arrived along with the drinks. As the audience dug in there came a few housekeeping announcements. Then Sheriff Miller led Christman to the podium and introduced him with a word about the case he'd helped with. Christman spoke for less than a minute listing what he could do for any department on the cyber-crimes front.

Finally Jerome Cobbins plugged the museum and the cooks just as the main course appeared. Then he started regional a slide-show that ran throughout the meal.

"Now for some candid shots of all the Poplar Park candidates," called Cobbins from his table as dessert arrived. The Harvard Graphics interface appeared on the screen briefly as the technician brought up a different show.

First up came pictures of a blocky man, seated two tables over from Reynolds, fishing. Fishing in rivers. Fishing in lakes. Fishing in the ocean. Finally a slide saying, "Enough Fishing, Already!"

Then McTeal appeared playing softball, coaching for the Police

Athletic League and at the Golden Gloves. Hoots of laughter sprang up at some grainy video frame grabs as McTeal tackled a suspect into a huge vat of ping-pong balls. His dark African face and hands made an incredible contrast to both the balls and the dressed in white suspect's florid skin.

The other candidates' followed until only Sarah Mitchell remained. First came a shot of her competing in a collegiate gymnastics meet. Next she danced at hot night spot. Out of the corner of his eye Reynolds watched her smile slightly, but she seemed tense.

Now came pictures following her on some kind of business errand. She drove to a city park, then headed down a secluded walking trail. Reynolds saw the woman's face tighten as each new slide appeared.

On that trail she met someone wearing a hooded sweatshirt. Items changed hands. Next came a blowup of the hooded man's face. And a label, "Leo Schmidt, of the Central East Drug Ring." Shots of banking records followed, plus pictures of Mitchell opening the door of a personal storage unit.

The elevator music accompanying the earlier slides faded away. Then words came. Words that constantly changed pitch and tone. Words that bounced off the walls of the meeting room like gunfire.

"Sarah Mitchell! These pictures, and other evidence, are now in the hands of your department's Internal Affairs Command. Copies are also on the way to the D.E.A. and the Governor's office."

The room's lights dimmed, but a narrow spotlight centered on Mitchell's chair brightened. This time Reynolds did not jump when the words continued.

"You have one chance before everything comes crashing down on you. Go home. Turn yourself in. Now!"

Reynolds watched as the woman swallowed. All color had long since drained from her face. Slowly she retrieved her purse from the floor. Pushing back her chair she walked to the exit. The sound of her high heels echoed around the room until the door closed. Reynolds started breathing again, but kept his hand near his Glock.

The Chief of the City's Department stepped to the podium.

"For those of you new to the region," he began, "that was the man known as the Voice. If anybody else has serious skeletons in your closets, he *will* find them. You may never knowingly meet the Voice, but…"

**Later on the night of the Metro Police Chiefs' Association Meeting**

Finally reaching home after midnight Agent Reynolds found his wife and two boys sound asleep. No surprise.

He tossed his bag of holiday goodies from the party on the kitchen table as he debated on a nightcap. Finally he decided he was still too wired to even try to sleep. Pouring himself a glass of milk he pulled the comb-bound film script out of the bag.

As he had reached the door of the museum on the way out, Christman buttonholed him.

"What I said before about my script was for public consumption. I wrote it with a specific local, very low budget, production house in mind. Fact is, every scene with Lt. Simmons and me, or with me and the Voice, is as close to what really happened as I could safely make it. But who'd believe it?"

Reynolds took a sip of milk and opened the script. He flipped past the page of legal boilerplate and began to read...

# A VOICE FOR JUSTICE

FADE IN FROM CREDITS TO CITY SHOT

SUPER:  Summer 1993

FADEIN TO HANDS TYPING AT A COMPUTER KEYBOARD  THIS IS MR. M'S OFFICE. A TV NEWSCAST PLAYS IN THE BACKGROUND.

NEWSCASTER: ...this makes another confrontation in the Middle East almost a certainty. In local news, Channel Five has learned, exclusively, that the Metro-Urban Commission is expecting at least eight bids on the area wide Fiber-Optic Highway by the Thursday deadline. In addition to expected bids by communications giants like A.T. & T., several groups of smaller companies are rushing to put together packages for this state of the art data transfer system. Lorna Jefferson is standing by, live, with a spokesman for one of these alliances. Lorna…

AS LORNA BEGINS TO SPEAK, JOHNNY (MR. M'S GOFER) BURSTS IN WAVING A VIDEOTAPE.

JOHNNY: Hey, Mr. M. Johnson just sent this tape over. He thinks you'll want to look at it right away.

MR. M IS VERY IRRITATED AT BEING INTERRUPTED LIKE THIS. HE GLARES AT THE COMPUTER SCREEN, THEN COMPOSES HIMSELF BEFORE HE TURNS TO JOHNNY.

MISTER M: Very well, let's see if Johnson is justified. The news is being taped in another room. Run it in that VCR, Johnny.

SUDDENLY REALIZING HE MIGHT BE IN TROUBLE, JOHNNY MEEKLY PUTS THE TAPE IN THE VCR. THE NEWSCAST CONTINUES AS THE TAPE CUES ITSELF.

LORNA: …as you know, the Fiber-Optic Highway would put our whole area at the cutting edge of the Information Age. The Metro Area could be a Worldwide data hub…

THE TAPE WAS SHOT FROM A PARKED CAR. IT BOBS AND WEAVES LIKE MUCH AMATEUR VIDEO. JOHNSON BEGINS WITH A VOICEOVER. THE TAPE SHOWS A CAR DRIVE UP. CHRISTMAN GETS OUT OF THE PASSENGER SIDE CARRYING A FLIGHT BAG. GRANT EMERGES FROM A NEARBY DOOR AND SHAKES CHRISTMAN'S HAND. THEY CHAT A MOMENT BEFORE THEY GO INSIDE.

JOHNSON: Billy's coming back. He's been gone long enough to make a run to the airport. (PAUSES) Don't know who this guy is, but for Grant, this is the royal treatment.

MR M STOPS THE TAPE AND BACKS IT UP TO A FREEZE-FRAME OF THE CLOSEST SHOT OF CHRISTMAN. HE LAUGHS.

MISTER M: Those high-tech idiots. They've attracted more attention than I'd realized. What a joke!

JOHNNY: Gee, Mr. M. I thought you were mad at them for hiring away some of our guys.

MISTER M: I certainly am mad, but they've just handed me the answer to our problem with them. That's Michael Christman, the Hacker Cop. He's one of the few people in law enforcement with the devious mind and the technical skills to really give us a problem. Hummm. Johnny, didn't you say you know the man who sells Grant's group all their gear?

JOHNNY: Sure, Frank Smithers over at Sanders Electronics.

MISTER M: Good. You'll arrange for Smithers to tip Grant off, then we'll let the police know who knocked off their fellow cop. Those that don't take the fall will be too busy hiding to bother me. HA! Grant and his bosses have got the long term outlook of a purse snatching junkie. They want money now, when waiting a year or two could make them rich for life. Now their own stupidity will put them out of action. No one could stop this chain of dominoes once I push the first one.

FADEOUT. IF POSSIBLE, USE A SIGNATURE TRANSITION TO CHANGE SCENES TO ONE OF THE VOICE'S DRESSING ROOMS. HE IS SEEN AS AN OUTLINE APPLYING GOOP TO HIS FACE. FINALLY HE REACHES OUTSIDE THE SHOT AND PICKS UP A MASK OF PETERS' FACE WHICH HE STARTS TO PUT ON. FADEOUT.

FADE IN ON A HAND THAT PLACES A HISSING CYLINDER OF GAS IN AN AIR VENT. PULL BACK TO A SCENE OF A SCRUFFY REST ROOM. WHILE HE VOICES-OVER, THE VOICE REMOVES ITEMS FROM HIS CLOTHING. HE PUTS TOGETHER A GAS GUN AND PLACES A PISTOL IN HIS BELT. FLUSHING THE TOILET, HE EXITS.

VOICE (voice over): I hate cases like this. Dammit! You'd think I'd learn. Get the evidence. Get the information. Turn it over to the cops, to the prosecutor, to the media. Let them do their jobs…help them do their jobs. Don't do it for them. I'm tired. I'm dirty. My mask is a bad fit. (SMOOTHS HIS TEMPLES) But no! I've got to get in the middle of things, again! Why didn't I find a nice safe, calm, career…like training

Piranha at an Amazon Theme Park?

THE VOICE ENTERS AN OFFICE NEXT TO THE BATHROOM. IT HAS A THROWN TOGETHER LOOK. THREE TOUGHS ARE LOUNGING AROUND. CHRISTMAN IS TIED TO A CHAIR. HE APPEARS SOMEWHAT BATTERED. GRANT, OBVIOUSLY THE LEADER, QUESTIONS THE PRISONER. HE TURNS FROM THE CHAIR AS THE VOICE ENTERS.

GRANT: (SLAP) You think its got rough? (SLAP) You don't tell me your contact, you'll see rough! Hey, Peters…I almost sent a rescue party after you.

VOICE: (WHINING & UNHAPPY) Well, you picked the takeout food. (grabs stomach & grimaces) Ought to put out a contract on that cook. Be a public service. Don't any of you taste anything funny?

FIRST THUG: Yeah. My mouth tastes sort of metallic.

VOICE: Mine did right before I headed for the can. What a mess! Just when we catch an undercover cop, we may all have food poisoning.

GRANT: That's no problem…

CUT TO SHOT OF VOICE RELEASING THROWING KNIFE FROM SLEEVE.

GRANT: Maybe we make him eat the leftovers. Nahhh! (raises gun, aims at cop) That'd take too long.

THE VOICE HALF TURNS, AND THROWS KNIFE. GRANT DROPS GUN & GRABS AT KNIFE IN THE SHOULDER. SIMULTANEOUSLY, THE VOICE YANKS OUT GAS GUN AND SPRAYS THREE THUGS. TWO DROP ALMOST INSTANTLY, THE THIRD DRAWS A GUN. THE VOICE SWINGS GAS GUN RIGHT TOWARDS GRANT, WHILE HE DRAWS AND FIRES PISTOL. THE THIRD THUG IS THROWN BACK AGAINST THE WALL. THE VOICE TURNS AND CONFRONTS GRANT. SLIPPING THE GAS GUN IN HIS POCKET HE STEPS UP TO THE TEETERING GRANT. THE VOICE HITS HIM WITH AN OPEN HANDED THRUST.

GRANT FALLS WITH A CRASH. THE VOICE SPRAYS EACH CROOK WITH MORE GAS. HE COLLECTS THEIR GUNS, THEN TURNS TO THE BOUND MAN.

VOICE: Where did they bring you in from? I know most of the local undercovers.

CHRISTMAN: I'm Mike Christman from Lancing, Michigan. Who the heck are you? I sure didn't eat, but I taste something metallic, too. Did you poison us, somehow?

VOICE: Its a binary gas. I flooded the place with one part from the bathroom. Takes most people out with the first whiff of the other component. I sure didn't want to take on all four of them if I didn't have to. (REACHES BEHIND CHRISTMAN) I'm going to untie you most of the way. These clowns will be out at least half an hour. You'll be loose in a couple of minutes.

CHRISTMAN: Wait a minute… I thought you were a local cop. What are you? Special Fed Strike Force?

WHILE CHRISTMAN SPEAKS, THE VOICE TURNS AWAY AND ADJUSTS HIS VOICE BOX. HE LAUGHS BRIEFLY.

CHRISTMAN: (ASTONISHED AT THE WEIRD LAUGH) What the…?

SPEAKING IN HIS OUT OF THIS WORLD VOICE, THE VOICE PICKS UP AND DIALS THE TELEPHONE ON THE BATTERED DESK.

VOICE: Let me speak to Simmons. (PAUSES) Ho, Simmons, guess who? Yeah, right. Listen, I'm at 4897 Tracy-Dee Way. Some characters caught an undercover. Nahh, he's okay. Just ticked off. You got four sleeping beauties. See you.

THE VOICE HANGS UP AND TURNS TO CHRISTMAN. HE RUBS HIS TEMPLES.

VOICE: Help is on the way. Simmons is a good cop. Trust her. I don't know who blew your cover, but you sure need to find out. Good luck.

(EXITS)

CHRISTMAN: Wait a minute…Who *are* you??..

FADE OUT. THE FOLLOWING SEQUENCE OF THE VOICE IS INTERCUT WITH THE CONVERSATION BETWEEN SIMMONS AND CHRISTMAN. THE VOICE LEAVES THE BUILDING, GETS IN A CAR, WAITS FOR A POLICE CAR TO GO BY, THEN DRIVES OFF. HE DRIVES TO A HOUSE, AND USES AN AUTOMATIC GARAGE DOOR OPENER TO ENTER. THE DOOR CLOSES. IN THE GARAGE THE VOICE SETS AN ALARM SYSTEM AND ENTERS THE BASEMENT. HE SITS AT A MIRRORED MAKEUP TABLE. THE LIGHTING LEAVES HIM IN SILHOUETTE. HE STRIPS OFF HIS MASK AND WIG AND TOSSES THEM INTO A MORE LIGHTED AREA. HE APPLIES CREAMS AND LOTIONS TO HIS FACE. HE RISES TO STRETCH. HE ENTERS A DARK BEDROOM AND CRAWLS IN BED. FADEOUT.

AT THE OFFICE THE LAST OF THE REVIVED CROOKS IS HAULED AWAY. CHRISTMAN AND SIMMONS SIT AROUND THE DESK.

VOICE (voice over): I stayed close until Simmons arrived with lots of backup. As I pulled out I wondered just what she'd tell Christman about me.

RADIO NEWSCAST (AS THE VOICE SITS IN MAKEUP CHAIR): And in other news… The city's schools get a report card. Speculation grows about the number and cost of the bids due Thursday for the areas massive Fiber Optic Data Highway.…

CHRISTMAN: I know this sounds crazy, Lt. Simmons. I mean this guy seems unreal…

SIMMONS: Oh he's real enough, all right. Mostly we call him The Voice. The reason should be obvious. Officially, he pretty much doesn't exist. He never seems to be the same person twice. Anyone on the force hears stories about him. Most people never knowingly see or hear him. Take my case. When I made detective I ran into some of the the force's good ol' boys. They just didn't want me around. I also picked up a snitch.

He fed me a lot of good material. His information on a loan shark operation helped get me my promotion to sergeant. The good ol' boys crawled back into the woodwork. Five years later I'm up the creek, like you were. My snitch shows up like the U.S. Cavalry. After he takes down the bad guys, I find out he's The Voice. Now he usually calls me with that graveyard voice turned on. Gives me the shivers. I feel like a five year old in a haunted house. He's a legend, you know. Some of the stories about him you couldn't sell to a comic book. Hell, so many people owe him…Plus he makes a point of finding evidence on crooked cops and politicians.

CHRISTMAN: You mean he's a vigilante?

SIMMONS: Not the way most people mean. He's not out to settle everything on his own. Thank God! Not one of those hit-and-run commandos who try to wipe out whole organizations. He told me once he wants to make the system work better. If these jerks had decided to wait until tomorrow to deal with you, he'd have slipped out and called us. As it was…

CHRISTMAN: Yeah! He came thru for me. (PAUSES) What did you mean about being different people?

SIMMONS: At one time or another he's appeared as White, African, Asian, Native American, even once or twice as a fat lady. Peters, the guy he played here…probably a prime example. He'll turn up sedated in a motel or something. (PAUSES) A few years ago our professional politico former Mayor went on a TV talk show with a distinguished shyster and his boss, a big developer. Suddenly His Honor sprouts a backbone and accuses the developer of bribery, graft and unsafe building practices. The lawyer gets mad and ugly. Suddenly, on live TV mind you, Hizhonor drop kicks the mouthpiece right off the set. Turns out the real Mayor was two hundred miles away. He spent the week fishing with a bunch of FBI, Treasury Agents, and Secret Servicemen. His Honor quietly retired. The lawyer and his bosses are doing fifteen to twenty at Leavenworth.

EXIT AND FADEOUT.

FADE IN TO THE SIMMONS' OFFICE AT THE POLICE STATION. SIMMONS AND CHRISTMAN ENTER WITH COFFEE CUPS. SOME

TIME HAS PASSED. CHRISTMAN'S FACE HAS BEEN CLEANED AND PATCHED.

SIMMONS: You turned down the doctor's offer of pain killer... Want something stronger in your coffee?

CHRISTMAN: I'm not hitting the street anytime soon. What ya' got?

SIMMONS: (TAKING FANCY PERFUME BOTTLE OUT OF DESK) Just Vodka. (TOPS OFF CUP) Now, before intelligence finds you, tell me how you ended up-up the creek on my turf. For once I'd like to be in on something before it blows up around here.

CHRISTMAN: Well, normally... What the Hell! The guy who saved my butt said to trust you...

SIMMONS: That's nice to hear.

CHRISTMAN: Seems my name fell out of one of those special databases the Feds keep. My hobby is computers. Computer programming for one thing. I've also worked on computer crime and illegal use of communications systems. The guy who briefed me was Justice Department. He said another agency needed to place a computer person. Seems underworld talent hunters had been hiring crooks with communications backgrounds. Well, they set me up as a guy who just beat a big hacking rap. I did an interview in Dallas, then they sent me here. I don't know when they got on to me. I reported to the clowns you locked up. Its obvious they aren't hi-tech. They barely know which end of the phone to talk into. The Voice, as Peters, joined us last night. I guess he'd (I mean Peters) just finished up an assignment for the higher ups. Anyway, this morning we went to that office and I got jumped. They knew I was undercover. I guess they'd been told if I didn't talk quickly to get rid of me. You know the rest.

SIMMONS: Did they know who you are?

CHRISTMAN: They knew exactly what I was. That includes my background in commo and computers. I don't think they had my name or hometown, but they didn't have any doubts, either.

SIMMONS:   Curiouser and curiouser. I guess you'd better call your contact.
(FADE OUT)

FADE IN TO THE VOICE'S BEDROOM. HE IS ONLY SHOWN IN SILHOUETTE. HE SITS UP, STRETCHES & HEADS FOR THE SHOWER. HE DRESSES AND GOES TO THE KITCHEN. MOST EVERYTHING IN THE REFRIGERATOR HAS SPOILED. HE USES FROZEN ITEMS AND CANS TO MAKE A RATHER GRIM MEAL. HE DRESSES, PUTS ON A NEW FACE AND LEAVES IN THE OTHER CAR IN THE GARAGE. HE DRIVES UP TO A PAY PHONE AND PUNCHES A NUMBER. SHOW A MONTAGE OF PHONES THAT RELAY THE CALL AROUND TOWN.

VOICE (voice over):  It felt good to spend a night without a mask. I'll put another on soon enough…Oh, Hell!  I meant to clean out the Fridge a week ago. Yuk! Oh, well, microwave breakfast with yummy vitamin shake. One of life's real pleasures. Let's see. Changed the face. Changed the outfit. Set the voice. Checked the weapons. Got to call George.

CUT TO AN OFFICE WITH LOTS OF COMPUTER AND COMMUNICATIONS GEAR. GEORGE SANCHEZ ENTERS AND PICKS UP THE PHONE.

GEORGE:  Communications Solutions and Security. Sanchez.

VOICE:  V., George. Can you talk?

GEORGE:  Sure. Change now.

GEORGE THROWS A SWITCH ON A BOX NEAR HIS PHONE. THE VOICE CLIPS SOMETHING TO THE RECEIVER CORD.

VOICE:  Scramble on?

GEORGE:  Scramble on. What's cooking?

VOICE:  I wish I knew, George. Someone's trying to bring in technicians with a shady background. Seem to be looking for both communications and computer experts. Somebody in the matrix has heavy duty connections to law enforcement information. Good enough to get a very quick fix on an out of the area undercover cop. What I'm picking up on the street doesn't make much sense...

GEORGE: How so?

VOICE: Some are looking for new technical people. Others seem to want to know about technicians who arrived recently and what they plan on doing.

GEORGE: Sounds like maybe two rival groups.

VOICE: That's one possibility. But if that's true, I'll bet there are two different goals involved. George, what I'd like you to do is eavesdrop on the computer nets and bulletin boards. Round up anything that seems funny to you. But for heavens sake, take extra precautions. I gather somebody involved in this thing is very, very good. You know how to reach me.

GEORGE: You be careful, too. I'll see what I can find.

GEORGE HANGS UP THE PHONE AND LAUNCHES A PROGRAM ON THE NEARBY COMPUTER. FADEOUT.

FADEIN TO A CORRIDOR IN THE POLICE STATION. SIMMONS LEANS AGAINST THE WALL WAITING. CHRISTMAN OPENS A DOOR AND STEPS INTO THE CORRIDOR. HE APPEARS VERY IRRITATED. HE WALKS OVER TO SIMMONS.

SIMMONS: Not too productive, I take it?

CHRISTMAN: Jerks! I mean... well... the local guys kept to the point, but those Federal types on the conference call spent most of the time asking questions about the Voice. For crimminy sakes! Someone just blew their perfect undercover operation and they want a detailed description of a phantom shape-shifter.

SIMMONS: If they start that again, refer 'em to the Secret Service's Presidential Detail. That's his best federal connection I know about.

CHRISTMAN: The Secret Service. He does get around.

SIMMONS: He's got more connections than…well…never mind. Did you get an assignment?

CHRISTMAN: No. I got told to sit tight. Don't do any legwork on my own. Well, I'll stay put, but I'm going to let my fingers do a lot of walking. I need to find a computer with a high-speed modem. None of the PC's I've seen here are any good at multi-tasking.

SIMMONS: What do you need that kind of capability for?

CHRISTMAN: I'm going hacking into every data base and bulletin board in this town and some beyond. Remember I told you about my specialty. I'll download the software I need from my home system. My custom system has four processing units running in parallel. This computer will have to run the modem, analyze the data that comes in, check for computer viruses and worms, plus keep the protection program running full bore.

SIMMONS: Protection program?

CHRISTMAN: It checks to see if someone is trying to trace your line, or read over your shoulder while you're on line. I'll modify a pay phone circuit down the road for the actual connection. By the time anyone can trace to the pay phone I'll be automatically off line and untraceable. I just have to get a good computer.

SIMMONS: Maybe I can help. Could you use a Linux system?

CHRISTMAN: My software's in ANSI Standard C language, platform independent. I can compile it about anywhere  What kind of power?

SIMMONS: My um… former significant other… long story… happens to be a slightly crazed computer artist. You know special effects, ray tracing. His newest box… he almost recites it like an litany. Fifty megahertz 68060 processor, math co-processor, sixty-four megabytes of 32bit RAM,  etc, etc. Fortunately we stayed good friends. Will that system work?

CHRISTMAN: Like a charm! When can I meet him?

SIMMONS: Let's go for a walk. We'll call him from a pay phone. With this kind of high tech monkey business, I'm not taking any chances. I'll arrange for you to meet him at the local comic book shop.

THEY WALK DOWN THE HALL AND VANISH AROUND THE CORNER. FADEOUT.

EXTERIOR DAY IN FRONT OF CLINTS COMICS. CHRISTMAN AND ANOTHER MAN EXIT. CHRISTMAN IS LOOKING IN A COMIC WITH A BEFUDDLED EXPRESSION. THE OTHER MAN LEADS HIM TO A CAR. THEY GET IN AND DRIVE OFF. FADEOUT.

INTERIOR DAY. FADEIN AS CHRISTMAN AND FRIEND ENTER A ROOM DEDICATED TO COMPUTING. FOLLOW WITH A BRIEF MONTAGE OF CHRISTMAN GETTING A BRIEFING ON THE COMPUTERS. THE LESSON OVER, CHRISTMAN SETTLES IN TO WORK.

MONTAGE OF CHRISTMAN AND SANCHEZ WORKING THEIR KEYBOARDS AND MICE. INTERCUT THIS WITH THE VOICE GOING IN AND OUT OF PLACES WITH HIS NEW FACE. LATER HE DRIVES TO A RUNDOWN COMMERCIAL STRUCTURE. LEAVING HIS CAR INSIDE, HE TAKES POSSESSION OF A VERY NONDESCRIPT FULL SIZE VAN. A CURTAIN OR PARTITION BEHIND THE DRIVERS SEAT ALLOWS NO VIEW OF THE REAR AREA. THE VOICE ENTERS THE REAR AREA ONLY TO RE-EMERGE WITH ANOTHER WARDROBE AND FACE. HE DRIVES OFF, PARKS, AND MAKES FURTHER INQUIRIES. HE PARKS IN A SECLUDED AREA AND CHANGES AGAIN. THIS CONTINUES AS NEEDED FOR THE EDITING PROCESS.

VOICE (voice over): I spend most of my time gathering information for somebody else to act on. When I dig for my own use, and on a deadline, I get mighty impatient. To speed things up I picked up my rolling dressing room. Years ago George Sanchez nick-named it the Imagemaker. The van stands out more than I like, but it puts more faces in play.

SANCHEZ AND CHRISTMAN BEGIN CROSSING EACH OTHER'S TRAILS ON THE BBS's AND DATA BASES. THE VOICE PHONES GEORGE.

GEORGE: That's right. I'm cross connected to some of Ma Bell's reserve lines. The kind they only activate for big emergencies and telethons. Any trace stops at the main phone company hub. I haven't been on some of these Boards in a long time, but my handle is solid, at least locally.

VOICE: Have you found anything promising yet?

GEORGE: Well, there are a few new boards that demand passwords as soon as you connect. Use'd to be you could at least get a number to call a human. I'm sure at least one involved a phone relay.

VOICE: I'll take down a list and try to trace them. Anything else?

GEORGE: A couple of things. Some really strange messages on public boards. Some seem to be partly tech and part prison slang. The more important thing is that I seem to have competition. A short time after I logged on I starting crossing trails with someone looking for the same stuff I am. I've spotted his trail a dozen times. He's probably seen mine as well.

VOICE: Any idea who?…

GEORGE: He's using a screen name with a national reputation in Hacker's circles. If he's the original, he's real good. I'll bet nothing short of 256bit encryption slows him down. I get the impression he's in town, but not from here. Does that help?

VOICE: I've got an idea who it might be. I'll try to check it out later. Great job! Now I'm ready to take notes.

CUT TO SCENE OF MR. M'S OFFICE. HE IS SEATED AT A COMPUTER. HE SPEAKS TO AN ASSOCIATE. (COULD BE HIS DRIVER, HIS NUMBER ONE OR HIS BIMBO.)

MISTER M: Well, these two do get around, don't they. Looks like they may find the competition for me. Too bad we can't take that chance.

GOON: We going after both of them, Mr. M?

MISTER M: I wish we could. That first person...male or female...has been around since modems were acoustic. I've tried off and on for years to trace him. Either he's in it for the thrills, or he's someone's Burbank.

GOON: Burbank, Boss?

MISTER M: An old saying. The communications man for someone. This hot-shot has been around just about as long as The Voice.

GOON: You mean we could be tangling with The Voice? That don't sound too good.

Mr. M.: What are you worried about? The Voice only goes after fools who act like Bonnie and Clyde. He hits a few drug dealers, big deal. Chances are he's after these idiots who want to run Vice info lines and raid Automatic Teller Machines. Anyway, we've got to put these peanut brained hoods down before they mess up our way into the fiber optic network.

GOON: Still, it sounds like they could make some bucks.

MISTER M: Well, yes, but they think small. Remember all the old cartoons of the fox raiding the chicken coop. If the fox can dodge the buckshot and the new fences, he eats pretty good. But what happens if the fox goes to the farmhouse first and takes out the farmer? He can get fat, for a while. But, if he's real smart he figures how to get inside the farmer's operation. Then he steals the chickens and cooks the books so the farmer never knows anything's wrong. I get inside the fiber optics net from the ground up, nobody, especially some wacko talking cowboy like The Voice, will ever know I'm there. But the net's got to go up looking clean. That's why these two bit high-tech louts have got to go. Am I clear?

GOON: Hey, Mr. M., even I can figure it out when you put it like that. How about the other hacker?

MISTER M: Got to be Christman. Now he's digging hard and fast.

Fortunately, there are only a couple of places left to call before he needs to start over. I'm going to sit and wait for him. Let him spin his web, but I'll get a line on him!

FADE OUT

FADE IN TO CHRISTMAN AT THE COMPUTER. HE IS SCROLLING THRU A TEXT FILE. SUDDENLY THE SCREEN CHANGES. IN LARGE LETTERS, IT READS, "TRACE DETECTED. SYSTEM SHUTDOWN--NOW!" CHRISTMAN QUICKLY DISCONNECTS PHONE CORD FROM THE MODEM.

EXTERIOR SHOT OF CHRISTMAN AT PHONE BOOTH.

CHRISTMAN: Simmons. It's the out of towner. I've bailed out of your friend's place. Somebody damn good just tried to put a trace on me. (PAUSES) I just need to dig a couple of more places. (PAUSES) Yes, I can make it to where you dropped me. Can you bring me that fastest laptop we talked about?…Great!…No we'll figure out my new base after we meet. (CHRISTMAN HANGS UP PHONE AND EXITS)

CUT TO SHOT OF SIMMONS HANGING UP PHONE, CLOSELY FOLLOWED BY ANOTHER MYSTERIOUS DEVICE BEING DISCONNECTED. SHE PAUSES, THINKING. SHE WALKS TO A PAY PHONE IN ANOTHER PART OF THE BUILDING. ANOTHER PAUSE AND SHE DIALS.

ANSWERING MACHINE (*very* sexy female voice over): Ultimate Escort Service. How are you, today. If you have a touch-tone phone and are a new customer press one, now. If you have an account press two, now. Or stay on the line…(SIMMONS LOOKS DISGUSTED, THEN PRESSES #7*.)

SIMMONS: Mr. I. Jones, please go to the warehouse. Your Arc will be waiting. (SIMMONS HANGS UP AND EXITS.)

EXTERIOR. SIMMONS EXITS POLICE BUILDING, GETS IN CAR AND DRIVES OFF. ANOTHER VEHICLE FOLLOWS. LONG STREET MONTAGE WITH A CLOCK OR TWO UNTIL SIMMONS PICKS UP CHRISTMAN. AN HOUR HAS PASSED. THE OTHER

VEHICLE FOLLOWS. FINALLY CHRISTMAN IS DROPPED OFF AT A RUNDOWN HOTEL. THE TAIL VEHICLE PARKS. THE DRIVER HEADS FOR A PHONE.

CUT TO SCENE OF SMALL NERVOUS MAN IN A SMALL OFFICE MARKED "SANDERS ELECTRONICS." A BIG, TOUGH MAN ENTERS.

NERVOUS MAN (Smithers):   Teddy,... You're early! I don't have everything ready.

Teddy:  Hey, what's a few minutes between friends. You're right, though. Your payment isn't due until the top of the hour. (GLANCES AT CLOCK THAT SAYS :45 OR :46.)  Will you be ready?

SMITHERS: (VERY NERVOUS) Well, I haven't counted...

Teddy:  Well, I'm not on the boss's clock yet. Don't tell no one, but I've got a new sideline. Information. You sell a lot of computers and modems and exotic commo gear. I need names dates and places.

SMITHERS:  (EVEN MORE NERVOUS) I could get in trouble...

Teddy:  How much trouble you think you're in if you don't pay on the hour?  I'll bet you even know what it'll take to pay off your whole note today. Am I right?

SMITHERS:  About $2700.

Teddy:  (VERY PLEASED)  Ya see. (PULLS OUT ENVELOPE AND COUNTS) Twenty-three, twenty-four, twenty-five, twenty-six, twenty-seven. I get the right info, you're clear with the boss. Anything you've moved in the last three months that smells, even a little. Got it!

SMITHERS:  (PAUSES) I'll have to make some copies. Be right back.

TEDDY FIDGETS WHILE THE CLOCK MOVES TO :58. SANDERS RE-ENTERS.

Sanders:  That should be everything. Please don't let this get out!

Teddy: (TAKING STACK OF PAPERS) Tell you what, Smithers, I ain't even been here yet. (HANDS OVER MONEY) I'm going out the door. When I come back in, I'll never bring it up again and you never mention it to me. Deal?

SMITHERS: (RELIEVED) Deal!

THE VOICE, AS TEDDY, EXITS QUICKLY. HE DODGES UNDER COVER JUST AS THE REAL TEDDY STOMPS DOWN THE HALL TO SANDERS ELECTRONICS' DOOR. TEDDY THROWS THE DOOR OPEN.

Teddy: Okay, Smithers, ready to pay up?

THE VOICE LEAVES HIS COVER WITH A SHAGGY WIG PULLED OVER HIS HEAD. HE REACHES IN HIS POCKET TO REMOVE A SILENT VIBRATING PAGER. DONNING SUNGLASSES, HE RUSHES TO A PAY PHONE.

VOICE (voiceover): On Time Teddy, the Collector. More predictable than the tide. (NOTICES BEEPER.) Oh, boy! Now…what?

CUT TO SHOT OF CHRISTMAN SEATED IN GRUBBY HOTEL ROOM. HE PECKS AWAY AT A LAPTOP COMPUTER. THE BAD GUYS GET THE DROP ON HIM. <TO BE WORKED OUT ON THE SET. DOWN FROM ROOF, IN FROM FIRE ESCAPE, THRU THE HEATING DUCTS OR WHATEVER MAY WORK WITHOUT HAVING CHRISTMAN LOOK TOO STUPID.> AS THE BAD GUYS GET SET TO DRAG CHRISTMAN OUT, A HOTEL EMPLOYEE APPEARS.

EMPLOYEE (a bit stoned): Hey, man, can you sort of hold it down? A couple of people on this floor work nights. Old George is one hundred and two. He can't fall asleep when he hosts in the Juice Bar, can he?… (NOTICES GUNS) Say, man I hope you got a license to sell those things. We run a clean dump here…

OF COURSE THE EMPLOYEE IS THE VOICE. HE CUTS LOOSE IN A BRAWL LIMITED BY THE STUNT ABILITY OF THE CAST AND

THE FRAGILITY OF THE SET. HE AND CHRISTMAN PREVAIL. AS THEY HAUL OFF THE GROUP LEADER AND RUSH TO THE IMAGEMAKER THEY TALK.

VOICE: Its me, Peters. Understand?

CHRISTMAN: After you busted that guy's sternum I decided that might be a good bet. How in the world did you find me?

VOICE: Simmons decided not to take any chances with tapped phones. She and I have used this fleabag for meetings, witness protection and whatnot...

CHRISTMAN: Whatnot? What kind of whatnot?

VOICE: Not the kind a dirty minded cop usually thinks of. She thinks we've been strictly professional.

CHRISTMAN: She thinks!!?

VOICE(Grinning): Guess you'll be the one to break the news... A few years ago I was perfecting a South American character. I needed to see how it played with a W.A.S.P. audience. I figured she'd be the most likely non-Hispanic female I knew to spot anything funny. Anyway I arranged to meet her and took her dancing. Tell her that Don Adolpho says she does an excellent Samba.

CUT TO SCENE OF MR. M PLAYING WITH SOME HIGH TECH ITEM. THIS IS HIS RECREATION. HE DOES NOT LIKE TO BE INTERRUPTED. JOHNNY ENTERS AND WAITS TO BE NOTICED.

MISTER M (exasperated): Yes, Johnny, *what* is it?

JOHNNY: Boss, Frank's team didn't check in on time. I didn't want to bother you, so I went down to that hotel. The barber next door's a bookie. I got my hair trimmed and put down a bet or two and asked how things 'd been going. Leo, that's the barber, told me there'd been some kind of ruckus. The cops came, but they didn't haul off anyone. I checked front and back. None of our guys were watching the place. I hope that was the right thing to do.

MISTER M (looks irritated during story, but smiles at Johnny): No, Johnny, the right thing. In fact one of your better ideas. Frank is not one of my most trusted employees. Could he have been playing more than one game? Pass the word: Frank and his men are suspect. Hold them, without unnecessary harm, until we have a better explanation of the situation.

JOHNNY: You bet, boss.

JOHNNY EXITS. MR. M GLOWERS AND TURNS BACK TO HIS PROJECT. HIS MOOD HAS CHANGED FOR THE WORSE. AFTER A MOMENT HE PUTS THE PROJECT AWAY DISGUSTEDLY.

MISTER M: Can't I even trust my own bought and paid for staff anymore? What is the world coming to?

CUT TO SCENE OF THE IMAGEMAKER CRUISING THRU THE STREETS. FINALLY, IT RETURNS TO THE BUILDING THE VOICE PICKED IT UP FROM. THE VOICE AND CHRISTMAN HAUL FRANK, THE TEAM LEADER, OUT OF THE VAN. THEY PLOP HIM ON A COUCH, OR EASY CHAIR. THE VOICE GIVES HIM A SHOT. WHILE WAITING FOR THE TRUTH DRUG TO TAKE EFFECT, THE VOICE TAKES MEASUREMENTS AND MAKES SCANS OF FRANKS FACE.

CROSSFADE TO:

THE TIME IS SOMETIME LATER IN THE SAME BUILDING, BUT AT A DIFFERENT CAMERA ANGLE. THE VOICE MIXES TOXIC LOOKING CHEMICALS AS HE AND CHRISTMAN TALK. FRANK IS FLOPPED OFF TO THE SIDE WITH WHAT LOOKS LIKE A THICK FACE PEEL GLEAMING WETTLY. HE ALSO WEARS EARPHONES.

CHRISTMAN: What have you got him listening to?

VOICE: Restful, comforting sounds. Works with the drug mixture. Makes him feel he's in a safe environment he can trust.

CHRISTMAN:  Little does he know. How long…?

VOICE:  If we had the time, I'd let it run several hours. Frank probably should have called in by now. If Simmons was able to keep control of the play at the hotel it'll look like nobody got arrested for an hour or two yet. Just some guards in the room until the hoods come out of the gas and yell for a lawyer. We've got to make our next move before then.

CHRISTMAN:  Which is?

VOICE:  That depends on what Frank knows, and on how well he responds to this quick treatment. (PUTS DOWN CHEMICALS)  I'm as far as I can go for the moment. Take off the headset.

CHRISTMAN WALKS OVER AND REMOVES THE HEADSET. THE VOICE SITS DOWN NEAR FRANK.

VOICE:  Can you hear me Frank?

FRANK:  Yes…

VOICE:  You were sent to grab Christman?

FRANK:  Yes.

VOICE:  What were you going to do with him?

FRANK:  Call in. Get instructions.

VOICE:  Frank, who do you report to?

FRANK:  Palmer, Herman Palmer.

VOICE:  Is Herman Palmer your boss?

FRANK:  No, he's a cut out…and relay.

VOICE:  Is Palmer's really part of your organization?

FRANK:  No, he's like our post office.

VOICE:  Then who is your boss, Frank?

FRANK:  Don't know, really. He's sometimes called Mr. M. I've never seen him.

THE VOICE FUMBLES HIS CHEMICALS AND SWEARS IN SOME FAR EASTERN LANGUAGE. CHRISTMAN COMES OVER TO HIM. CUT TO CLOSEUP AS THEY SPEAK.

CHRISTMAN:  Say again?

VOICE:  You don't want to know.

CHRISTMAN:  You've heard of this Mr. M?

VOICE:  Only whispers. Supposed to be a real Gentleman Crook. A David Niven or James Mason, with a lot of Mr. Spock and Dr. Zarkov thrown in. His exact goals are unknown. Supposed to be calm, cool, and tough as an old saddle.

CHRISTMAN:  Let's see if he has any idea of the big picture. Frank, do you work only for Mr. M?

FRANK:  Yes, if I want to stay healthy.

CHRISTMAN:  What sorts of thing do you and your friends do for Mr. M?

FRANK:  When there's no action, we hang out and listen.

CHRISTMAN:  What do you listen for?

FRANK:  Anything about guys pulling jobs with computers and phone taps, stuff like that.

CHRISTMAN:  Frank, is there one topic that's more important, or comes up more often than any other in your orders, or in the questions Mr. M. asks?

FRANK: I guess...sure...that's it...We got to tell everything, every little detail about this fiber optic thing.

CHRISTMAN (EXCITED): Frank, was Grant interested in the fiber optic deal.

FRANK: Sure. Hired a couple of Mr. M's people away. Kept looking for guys that understood fiber technology. Mr. M. got real mad about it.

CHRISTMAN AND THE VOICE EXCHANGE SATISFIED GLANCES. THE VOICE PICKS UP A FACE MOLD AND PLACES IT OVER FRANK'S FACE.

VOICE: That's very good, Frank. Now please hold your breath for a moment. When I'm done you can give us a list of places Mr. M's people hang out...

FADEOUT.

FADEIN TO SHOT OF CHRISTMAN GETTING INTO PASSENGER SIDE OF THE IMAGEMAKER. THE VOICE, AS FRANK, DRIVES AWAY WHILE CHRISTMAN STUDIES A CITY MAP. AFTER A DRIVE ACROSS TOWN, THEY PARK IN AN ALLEY. THE VOICE GETS OUT AND LETS A HANDCUFFED CHRISTMAN OUT AT GUNPOINT. THEY SPEAK BRIEFLY BEFORE ENTERING THE BUILDING.

VOICE: Ready?

CHRISTMAN: I guess so.

VOICE: Remember, the contact lenses give some protection.

THEY ENTER THE BUILDING AND GO DOWN A SHORT CORRIDOR. THEY PAUSE AT A DOOR MARKED "HERMAN PALMER, VENDING MACHINES & VIDEO GAMES." THEY ENTER.

CUT TO INTERIOR OF PALMER'S OFFICE AND WAREHOUSE. THERE IS A DESK, A COUPLE OF TABLES, SOME CHAIRS AND

LOTS OF BOXES AND PACKING CRATES. PALMER LOUNGES BEHIND HIS DESK. SEVERAL TOUGH GUYS SIT AROUND OR PLAY CARDS. THE VOICE PUSHES CHRISTMAN IN THE DOOR. HE ENTERS AND PUTS AWAY HIS GUN.

VOICE:  Here you go, Palmer. Sorry it took so long.

PALMER:  (RECOVERING FROM SHOCK)  Good-good t' see you Frank...Say, when you didn't call in, Mr. M. got worried. (THREE HOODS MOVE TO BLOCK DOOR, OTHERS APPEAR READY TO GO FOR WEAPONS.)  He wants me to get a full report. And I guess after those other boys went over to Grant he don't want you going nowhere until he checks you out. Nothing personal, Frank.

WITH THE VOICE STANDING VERY STILL AT THE CENTER OF ATTENTION, NOBODY PAYS MUCH ATTENTION TO CHRISTMAN. HE SLIDES FOUR SMALL BALLS OUT OF HIS SLEEVES AND INTO HIS HANDS. HE POPS THE TRICK CHAIN OF THE HANDCUFFS AND THROWS THE BALLS DOWN. THEY ARE FLASH AND CONCUSSION BOMBS. AS THEY DETONATE, THE VOICE HITS THE FLOOR AND ROLLS. CHRISTMAN DUCKS, THEN THE BOTH WADE INTO THE CONFUSED CROOKS. FADEOUT WHEN THE FIGHT IS OVER.

FADE IN AT SCENE OF LAST BATTLE. SLEEPING BODIES ARE STILL SCATTERED AROUND. ZOOM IN ON VOICE AND CHRISTIAN SEATED AMID THE DEBRIS, MAKING NOTES.

CHRISTMAN:  Man did we get lucky.

VOICE:  With what we got off the modems and communication nets we seem to have a pretty complete table of organization, plus some of the locations. Now to shake the tree and watch the nuts fall.

CHRISTMAN:  You want to turn this stuff over to Simmons, or who?

VOICE:  I hate to say it, but there's no time. We've got to find out which of the bidders for the fiber optic net Mister M is backing. It might be a planted insider in more than one of the majors...or it could be a key sub-contractor who's involved with most of the bids. Whoever it is has got to be exposed before the bid deadline.

CHRISTMAN: What if we reveal what we've got?

VOICE: Some officials would take it seriously, but what could they do? There's no real proof of conspiracy even. Could be seen as some old grudge blowing up with finger pointing. Some other honest officials I could name would file our ideas with the last Bigfoot sighting.

CHRISTMAN: The square-round file thirteen!

VOICE: Correct! Now for the luggage and the trip to Alcatraz...What do we do next?

CHRISTMAN: We might get the bidding postponed.

VOICE: That gives them time to really go undercover and shuffle the key technical bad guys into different positions. Besides if this gets done right, the whole region benefits. Dammit, I'm tired of technical progress being sidetracked by greedy thugs with big ideas.

CHRISTMAN: You sound like you've seen this before.

VOICE: Unfortunately, yes. Years ago I shot it out with the H-8 radicals. They'd raided the Hardin Nuclear Plant. Now you can argue about atomic safety and I'll probably agree with you. But the human race gave up on nature's only known free lunch...the Breeder Reactor...not because of safety concerns. No, the world caved in because of loony-toons like Gaddafi and cold calculating crooks like Mr. M. Fiber optic communications doesn't have the safety issues, but we could still lose a lot of the benefits if the Mr. M's of the world get their foot in the door. (PAUSES) Christman, whatever comes next, we'd better part company. Your lawman's conscience might act up.

CHRISTMAN: Hold on! Mr. M's perps are gunning for me on sight. With what we know about his abilities, he's probably got my home address. I've got no desire to go the witness protection route. So, what comes next?

VOICE: When he fingered you he basically arranged to take out that rival gang. He wants a monopoly. With this info (HOLDS UP PAPERS) we just became his new, improved, truculent competition.

CHRISTMAN: So what's my part in this gang?

VOICE: Wheelman. This has got to be a bigger gang than just two. Take this map. We'll hit randomly. You drive, I'll change.

THEY GATHER UP PAPERS AND WEAPONS THEN EXIT. FADEOUT.

FADEIN TO A MONTAGE OF THE IMAGEMAKER BEING DRIVEN BY CHRISTIAN. EACH TIME THEY STOP, A DIFFERENT PERSON EXITS THE REAR OF THE VAN AND GOES INTO A TARGET BUILDING. IN THE CASE OF STOREFRONT OPERATIONS SOMEONE MAY COME FLYING OUT THE DOOR. THEY MAKE SEVERAL STOPS UNTIL THE VOICE EXITS THE VAN AS A BLACK MAN.

CHRISTMAN: (Surprised) That's right, Simmons said you did all races.

VOICE: Think about it, Christman. You've never seen one square inch of my real skin. What race, or races, am I?

CHRISTMAN (FLABBERGASTED): Hummm… Good question.

THE VOICE ENTERS AND EXITS THIS LOCATION. HE REENTERS THE VAN AND CHRISTIAN DRIVES OFF. AT THE NEXT STOP THE VOICE ENTERS AND STAYS A WHILE. CHRISTIAN KEEPS LOOKING AT HIS WATCH AND FINALLY ENTERS. HE CLIMBS THE STAIRS TO A LOFT. HE FINDS BODIES ALONG THE WAY. FINALLY HE DISCOVERS THE VOICE. HIS CLOTHES ARE A MESS AND PART OF ONE CHEEK OF HIS MASK IS MISSING. THE VOICE THROWS DOWN ON HIM AS HE ENTERS.

CHRISTMAN (STANDING VERY STILL): I started to get worried.

VOICE: A few more than I expected. Plus some loot worth having. Names dates and places. Looks like the honcho of this shop covered his bets. That's him in the closet. We'll haul him out to the Imagemaker. After all, he is our gang's leader. He planned all these attacks. Now he's going to make Mr. M an offer he's not supposed to refuse.

THEY HAUL THE HONCHO TO THE VAN AND TIE HIM IN A CHAIR. AS CHRISTIAN CLOSES THE DOOR THE VOICE IS MEASURING THE HONCHO'S FACE. CHRISTIAN DRIVES OFF.

SEVERAL HOURS HAVE PASSED. THE VOICE AND CHRISTMAN WORK OUT OF THE BACK OF SANDERS ELECTRONICS AS THE STAFF TAKES AN EXTENDED NAP. CHRISTMAN HAS PUT TOGETHER A RUBE GOLDBERG CONTRAPTION OUT OF COMPUTER COMPONENTS, RADIO PARTS AND WHATEVER ELSE THAT LOOKS GOOD. THEY BEGIN TO LEAVE MESSAGES FOR MR. M ON LOCAL BBS'S AND CHAT ROOMS. THE VOICE FINISHES THE MASK OF REVELL, THE CAPTURED SHOP BOSS. NOW CHRISTMAN GETS HIS FACE WORKED ON AS HE MONITORS THE JACK-LEG SYSTEM FOR ANY REPLIES. FIRST HE GETS A SHAVE. THEN THE VOICE APPLIES THE HORRID LOOKING BASE COAT OF MAKEUP. THE MONTAGE FADES OUT.

MR. M IS CHANNEL FLIPPING, GLANCING AT VARIOUS COMPUTER SCREENS, IGNORING HIS DINNER, AND GENERALLY IN A ROTTEN MOOD. JOHNNY ENTERS.

JOHNNY (cautiously): Boss… (a bit louder) Mr. M? Say boss, Archie sent this printout over. Came off a city planning chat-room you had me tell him about once. Said he thought some of it might be aimed at you.

MISTER M: We'll see. Archie is hardly the brightest candle in the chandelier. However he is diligent. That printout could not be less enlightening than everything I've seen for the last two hours.

MR. M TAKES THE PRINTOUT FROM JOHNNY. HE GOES TO HIS DESK AND TURNS ON A LAMP. HE SPEAKS AS HE SCANS THE PAPER. USING A MARKER HE SCRATCHES OUT SOME AREAS. HE PUTS QUESTION MARKS NEXT TO A COUPLE OF PASSAGES. FINALLY HE GRABS A HIGHLIGHTER AND MARKS EVERY PASSAGE BY THE HANDLE "Model Man."

MISTER M: That's fluff. So's that. Probably not him, or him. "Model Man?" Well he's got something to say. Archie may be right. This clearly refers to Grant's bunch. Model Man? Could be a hint.

Mr. M GOES TO A COMPUTER AND TYPES A SEARCH FOR "plastic model company names."

MISTER M: Serious stones, or stupid. I'm not sure. Vaughn Revell is one of our main suppliers of men and equipment. Johnnie, send Johnston's team to Revell's place. If he's there, makes sure he does not leave. I expect the place will be empty. Have him call the cutout number as soon as he can.

JOHNNY: Sure, boss. (exits)

MISTER M: So you want to be my partner, do you?

MR. M BEGINS TO MAKE NOTES AND TO COMPOSE A MESSAGE.

CUT TO INTERIOR SHOT OF PLACE VOICE PICKED UP IMAGEMAKER. CHRISTMAN HELPS LOAD BOXES AND WEIRD STUFF INTO IMAGEMAKER AND SMALL U-HAUL TYPE OF VAN. SOMETHING "PINGS" AT THE BACK OF THE SET. VOICE (AS REVELL) WALKS OVER TO TURN ON MONITOR. DEVICE WARMS UP TO DISPLAY TEST.

CHRISTMAN: Did he take the bait?

VOICE: Looks promising. Wants to set up a private chat-room.

CHRISTMAN (as he begins to work keyboard): Excellent! I'll send the parameters. And tell him it won't be ready until midnight so I can set up my electronic security.

VOICE: Fine, but then we'd better haul ass.

VOICE HANDS CHRISTMAN GLOVES. THEY BOTH PUT GLOVES ON BEFORE ENTERING VEHICLES. IMAGEMAKER AND TRUCK DRIVE OFF. FADEOUT.

THE TWO VEHICLES ARRIVE AT REVELL'S SOMEWHAT ISOLATED HOME. MONTAGE OF UNLOADING BOTH VEHICLES. THEN VOICE PUTS RENTED TRUCK IN GARAGE. THE IMAGEMAKER REMAINS OUTSIDE.

MONTAGE OF THE TWO MEN DRAWING ALL THE BLINDS AND CURTAINS, THEN SETTING UP VARIOUS DEVICES ON DOORS AND WINDOWS. THERE ARE SPOTLIGHTS, STROBE LIGHTS, SOME SPEAKERS. THEY PLACE GAS GRENADES AND FIRE EXTINGUISHER LIKE GAS DISPERSERS IN DIFFERENT ROOMS AND IN THE BACK YARD. IN ADDITION, THERE ARE DEVICES THE AUDIENCE WILL NOT RECOGNIZE.

VOICE: Did you get Revell settled?

CHRISTMAN: All set. Looks like he had a nightcap and hit the sack without a care in the world.

VOICE: Good. The sensors we put up should give us warning when Mr. M's goons, or anything larger than a basset hound, shows up. Now to set the electronic stage.

THE TWO REPLACE REVELL'S VERY BASIC COMPUTER SETUP WITH A STATE OF THE ART MACINTOSH WITH MODEM AND OTHER PERIPHERALS. THE MAC BEGINS PRE-PROGRAMMED SEARCHES ON THE LOCAL BBS'S THUS TYING UP THE HOUSE'S PHONE.

VOICE & CHRISTMAN TURN ON THE TV IN ONE ROOM. THE SET'S FLICKERING GLOW CAUSES SHADOWS TO FALL ON THE DRAWN BLIND.

AS IT IS APPROACHING FULL DARK BOTH MEN HANG INFRARED GOGGLES AROUND THEIR NECKS. THEY BEGIN WATCHING FOR TROUBLE. FADE OUT.

FADE IN TO A SHOT OF A SIDE ROAD. A LUXERY CAR AND TWO VANS QUIETLY PARK. THUGS FROM THE VANS GATHER AROUND MR. M. HE SENDS ONE CLIMBING A TELEPHONE

POLE CARRYING A LINEMAN'S PHONE. WITH SOME GESTURES MR. M INSTRUCTS THE MEN AS HE BREAKS THEM INTO THREE GROUPS. THE POLE CLIMBER RETURNS.

CLIMBER: Nothing but electronic sounds. And lots of 'em.

MISTER M: Very well. Head out on your assignments, men.

THE THREE GROUPS SPLIT UP AND HEAD TOWARDS REVELL'S HOUSE. AS THEY MOVE OFF MR. M INSTRUCTS HIS PERSONAL DRIVER.

MISTER M: Shoot anybody who approaches that you can't positively identify. Be ready to pull out immediately.

MR. M HEADS OFF IN THE SAME DIRECTION AS HIS MEN. FADE OUT.

FADE IN TO CHRISTMAN LISTENING TO HEADPHONES AS HE SITS BY THE COMPUTER.

CHRISTMAN: Vio… I mean Revell! Movement from the direction of that side road coming in on the parabolic mike.

VOICE (as Revell enters shot): Excellent. Phase two on the modem.

CHRISTMAN PLAYS WITH THE COMPUTER KEYBOARD. CUT TO SHOT OF THE SCREEN. REVELL'S SUPPOSED MESSAGE BEGINS TO APPEAR ONE SENTENCE AT A TIME.

MODEL MAKER (Revell's screen name): Something's wrong. Sounds like somebody's trying to break in.

MODEL MAKER: Emergency! Send police to 2215 Sidney in West Poplar Park. This must be about fiber optic net takeover. Uploading file to BBS. Read and act. If I live thru this I'll have more info…

THE CONNECTION IS AUTOMATICALLY BROKEN. THE DIAL TONE COMES UP ON THE COMPUTER SPEAKER. THE NUMERALS 9-1-1 APPEAR ON THE SCREEN.

911 OPERATOR: 911 Emergency. How may I help you?

THE CONNECTION IS BROKEN.

VOICE & CHRISTMAN ACTIVATE AN ARTICULATED SILHOUETTE OF REVELL TO THROW SHADOWS ON THE WINDOW OF HIS DEN/OFFICE.

CHRISTMAN: Only steal from the best, huh?

VOICE: Sure. But this is a heck of a lot more effective than Mrs. Hudson pushing a plaster bust on her hands and knees. Time for the infrared goggles.

BOTH MEN PUT ON THEIR GOGGLES AND BEGIN TO LOOK OUT THE EDGES OF DARKENED WINDOWS. A CROOK USING AN INFRARED SPOTLIGHT ALMOST BLINDS THEM WITH ITS BEAM.

VOICE (taking out a remote control device): Round one's a draw. (Pushes button.) Let's see what they make of this.

A MIST BEGINS TO RISE FROM DEVICES BELOW EACH WINDOW SILL. THE MIST CHANGES COLOR A BIT AS A CHEMICAL REACTION TAKES PLACE WITH THE AIR. TO THE MEN OUTSIDE THE WINDOWS GLOW. THIS MAKES THEIR INFRARED GEAR USELESS. ONE GROUP GATHERS AT THE FRONT DOOR. ANOTHER PREPARES TO KICK IN THE BACK DOOR.

CHRISTMAN (whispers into headset): Ready to breach the rear.

VOICE (also into headset): Front, also.

SHOT OF HANDS DOING THINGS WITH A COMPLEX PHONE SYSTEM.

911 OPERATOR: This is 911 operator six-seven.

POPLAR PARK DISPATCHER: Poplar Park, go.

911 OPERATOR: Poplar park. We have a call and immediate hang-up from 2215 Sidney, West Poplar Park. Unable to reestablish contact.

POPLAR PARK DISPATCHER: Understood 911 dash 67. 2215 Sidney, West P.P. Will check out.

CROSSFADE TO CROOKS AS THEY HIT BOTH DOORS.

CUT TO MR. M WATCHING FROM A DISTANCE. HIS DRIVER HURRIES UP AND IS ALMOST SHOT FOR HIS EFFORTS.

DRIVER: Marty just faxed this in, boss.

MR. M SNATCHES THE OFFERED PAPER. FACES AWAY FROM HOUSE TO USE HOME BREWED DIM RED LED FLASHLIGHT. HE FREEZES BRIEFLY AS THE MESSAGE ABOUT THE PLOT GOING UP ON BBS's ALL OVER TOWN SINKS IN.

MISTER M: (hisses): We've been set up! We're leaving.

DRIVER LOOKS BACK AT REVELL'S HOUSE BRIEFLY. THEN TURNS TO FOLLOW MR. M.

CUT TO SHOT OF POLICE CARS HEADING FOR THE AREA.

CUT TO SPLIT SHOT OF THE INTERIOR OF BOTH DOORS OF REVELL'S HOME. THE DOORS CRASH OPEN SIMULTANEOUSLY. THE CROOKS CHARGE IN TO BE MET BY CLOUDS OF THE VOICE'S GAS. THOSE THAT DO NOT GO DOWN IMMEDIATELY ARE HIT WITH TASERS OR FISTS HOLDING GUNS. (THE GUNS ARE NOT USED. BUT THE CROOKS DO GET A HARMLESS SHOT OR TWO OFF.)

NEAR THE FRONT DOOR THE IMAGEMAKER RELEASES A HUGE CLOUD OF GAS THAT TAKES OUT THOSE REMAINING OUTSIDE. AT THE BACK DOOR SEVERAL DISPERSERS ACHIEVE THE SAME RESULTS.

WITH ALL THE CROOKS APPARENTLY DOWN THE VOICE AND CHRISTMAN SLOWLY BACK UP IN THE HOUSE UNTIL THEY STAND BACK TO BACK.

CHRISTMAN: Ready for phase three?

VOICE: Let's get at it.

MONTAGE AS THE TWO CARRY THE CROOKS INSIDE AND ARRANGE AN ELABORATE SCENE AT THE BOTTOM OF THE STAIRS TO THE SECOND FLOOR. EACH CROOK IS HELD UP IN A POSITION FACING THE STAIRS, THEN HE IS SHOT WITH AN UNCHARGED TASER. HE IS THEN ALLOWED TO FALL. THEN THEY POSITION REVELL ON THE STAIRS AS IF HE HAS PASSED OUT FROM THE BRUISING HE GOT IN HIS ORIGINAL CONFRONTATION WITH THE VOICE. THEY LEAVE HIM WITH A MULTI-SHOT TASER IN EACH HAND. SOME EXPENDED TASERS LIE ON THE FLOOR AROUND HIM AND THREE MORE ARE ON THE SPECIAL BELT HE WEARS.

CHRISTMAN AND THE VOICE HEAR THE APPROACHING SIRENS AND LEAVE THE HOUSE.

CHRISTMAN: Fastest Taser in the Mid-West. (laughs, then pauses) Is that our exit cue?

VOICE: Darn right it is! Poplar Park may be a suburb, but the cops are good.

THE TWO HURRY OUTSIDE AND PILE INTO THE IMAGEMAKER. THE VOICE PULLS ACROSS THE FRONT LAWN AND HEADS AROUND TO THE BACK YARD. FADE OUT.

FADE IN ON CITY STREET CORNER. THE IMAGEMAKER PULLS UP. CHRISTMAN GETS OUT. HE TALKS TO THE VOICE THROUGH THE OPEN PASSENGER DOOR.

VOICE:  Here's where you get off, Christman. The Precinct's two blocks west. I'll call Simmons to expect you.

CHRISTMAN: How can I get in touch with you?

VOICE: You can't. Not directly. Call Simmons. Or leave messages on the local BBS's or chat rooms for 'Talker.'

FADE OUT. HOLD IN BLACK TO ESTABLISH THAT TIME HAS PASSED.

FADE IN. DAY. CHRISTMAN AND SIMMONS EXIT POLICE HEADQUARTERS. CAMERA FOLLOWS THEIR CONVERSATION AS THEY WALK THROUGH A PARKING LOT.

CHRISTMAN: Finally! I thought I'd end up swatting a Fed, or two.

SIMMONS: We're not scheduled to give depositions until next Tuesday. What's say we blow this town, copper?

CHRISTMAN: Sounds great to me. Any suggestions?

SIMMONS: Got the old family place on a private lake. Nobody but us, and the critters.

CHRISTMAN: Critters? That include birds? And bees?

SIMMONS: Could be. Want to find out?

CHRISTMAN OPENS THE CAR DOOR FOR SIMMONS. HE HURRIES AROUND TO JUMP IN.

CUT TO LONG SHOT OF CAR EXITING PARKING LOT. SHOT ZOOMS BACK AS CAR APPROACHES. CAMERA PANS AS CAR PASSES. PAN STOPS AND FOCUSES ON UNFAMILIAR MAN LEANING ON A MAILBOX. HE WATCHES THE CAR GO BY, THEN SMILES. HE REMOVES ONE OF THE VOICE'S THROWING KNIVES FROM HIS SLEEVE AND BEGINS TO CLEAN HIS FINGERNAILS.

FADE OUT TO CREDITS.

Reynolds washed out his milk glass. As he headed for bed he wondered how many other FBI Agents-In-Charge received volunteer help. Whether they wanted it, or not.

# Explosive Justice

by

Erwin K. Roberts
Based on Bowen Chadwick's Recounting

Chapter 1

## National News Net Reports

"Tonight on National News Net's *Focus America* for July 17, 1996... Tough Guys... Reel, Real, and Un-Real. Plus Countdown to the Olympics. Later in the program, Erwin K. Roberts interviews boxer Tommy Morrison and martial arts star Steven Segal. But right after this commercial break, a tough guy as hard to find as Bigfoot. Is he for real?"

Every time I play that tape I get goose bumps. Even after all these years. Just luck I recorded it. I'd delivered some sketches for a commission to the local NNN affiliate station boss. I stopped by to visit someone else I knew there. She told me to record that day's Focus America. "There's a local story that'll be a surprise for you and your buddies."

Since my home and my office, then as now, are the same thing, I just set both my VCR's and went on about the rest of my regular business. I visited the art supply house. Took some pictures of a possible location for a piece of work. Last, I checked in at Central Patrol. No sketches needed. Then I headed to Silo's

Silo's name has nothing to do with storing grain, or nuclear missiles. Fifty-some years ago Cyrus and Lois Hamstead founded the place. Cy-Lo's, get it? Probably the safest place in the city, at least sixty per cent of the clientele are armed at any given moment. Most of the ones with guns carry badges, too. A good chunk of the rest are Fire Fighters. Nobody messes with them either.

How did this come about? One of those ideas that looks great on paper, but doesn't pan out. In an effort to save money and offer all services in one convenient location, the city built a combination Police Station, Fire House, and city office building. The Central City Government Center opened just as the protests about the Viet Nam War cranked up. Every time someone's got a beef with one branch of the government, the other two get all the collateral action. Silo's was the only bar and grill in the area to survive that burst of urban redevelopment. Since, by then, Bart Olsen, a retired cop, owned it the emergency services soon adopted the place.

They'll never film a beer commercial at Silo's. Like everybody else, I go there to relax, unwind from the day's tensions, meet friends, and maybe have a pretty decent meal. None of those ninety mile an hour, everybody looks to be on speed, scenes. Thank heavens.

I walked in and let my eyes adjust. This early evening some of the booths and tables were full. The kitchen sounded busy. Two of my early pieces sit behind the bar. Tonight I couldn't see them because of three people standing at the turn of the "L" shaped bar, plus the bartender. Two of the three I knew, but the striking lady in the skirt and light jacket I sure didn't. Who I didn't know. What was as obvious as the small weapon, holstered FBI style, in the small of her back under her jacket. Arnie placed drinks as I approached.

"Ayy," said Arnie, "its the Prodigal Cop."

"Bowen," rumbled Sergeant Sam (for Samson) Jones, "that completes the chain of custody." Sam's normally precise English fools a lot of people into thinking he's some soft, suburban, college educated African-American. He can speak like a gang-banger, or even Buckwheat, if he wants, but has busted almost as many Philistines as his namesake.

"Custody, whose custody?" asked the short haired red-head. She had a face most men would call cute, but I caught a hint of steel in her large blue eyes.

"That's just Sam torturing the English language again," drawled Terry Faulkner "This is Bowen Chadwick, my former partner. Sam broke Bowen in. Bowen broke me in. I'm supposed to break you in. A bit more like four generations. Bowen, this is Megan McGregor. Technically she's a probie. But watch out, she used to be a Marine MP, or whatever they call it. Worked embassies, too."

"Some resume," I said as we shook hands. "All that and you'd be a perfect model for me."

"Wait a minute," she began guardedly, but there was humor in her eyes, as well. "I'd better tell you up front, I don't go out with other cops."

I covered my eyes in sorrow. "Not even reservists?" I asked.

"McGregor," began Sam, two octaves below James Earl Jones, "Bowen's no longer on the force full time. If you've seen him around the precinct, its because he draws suspects, both by hand and computer. His Damascus Road conversion to the fine arts didn't fully take. His main occupation deals with stone and molten metal these days. Those sculptures behind the bar are his."

She turned away to look at the pieces again. As she turned back she said, "All right, I get the hands with the hose nozzle. But the other one doesn't seem finished. Parts of a badge sticking out of raw rock?"

"You can't read the plate from here," I replied. "The title of the piece is 'Police Academy'…"

"Oh." She studied me to see if I was kidding. "And why, aside from the obvious, lascivious, reasons would I make a good model for you?"

"Two reasons. First, in addition to the excellent base body nature gave you, you are trained to a level where you have definition of muscles without the almost freakish look some of the female body builders obtain. Second you've been around places besides the fashion industry. I could see that from across the room. I wouldn't have to talk you out of any of those silly runway model poses or phony attraction ploys of centerfolds. Any questions?"

"I'm real, verses phony. You knew that in all of ten seconds. And blunt, too. Not bad," she said.

Terry chuckled at the exchange. "Bowen's usually straight ahead. I'll tell you some war stories tomorrow."

I glanced at my watch and asked Arny to bring up the NNN affiliate on the big TV over the bar.

"What cooks," asked Terry, "a docudrama about Rodan?"

"No, Terry, the Japanese still hold the rights to that name. Got a tip that N-Cubed's doing a local story."

We chatted for the next few minutes as I got to work on an Amber Boc. Of course they went to commercial after that teaser. We tried to guess what had attracted national attention.

Finally the host returned. "National News Net, a part of Heavens International Media, has a policy of leveling with our viewers. In our first story we're not sure of the accuracy of some of the material. Even some of our sources aren't sure whether what they've seen is correct or if they have been hoaxed. Curtis Van Loan has been working with our affiliate KQAZ on the story of the shadowy figure known as The Blaster..."

Samson's modulated bellow, "Everybody, quick! Story about the Blaster!" could have been heard a block away. His voice and the rush of people caused us to miss the first few words as Van Loan spoke facing the camera.

"...this city has a mystery, or perhaps more accurately, a mystery man. Some call him a hero, some a vigilante, some say he is a hoax. Whatever the case may be, everyone in town has an opinion about The Blaster."

I wonder how many people they had to point a camera at to get the stock answers you'd expect about something like this? The media created him to get ratings. He's what this city needs, something to scare the damn crooks and druggies. We don't know anything about him, he's too dangerous. Gheez! Stan Lee wrote better in the first year of "Spider-Man."

Van Loan continued, "When I came to town on an unrelated story, I began to hear things about The Blaster. Stories of a man popping out of nowhere who could blow things up by pointing at them. A man whose presence caused guns to misfire. A man who rescued people and subdued criminals before the police could arrive. A man who then pulled a Lone Ranger style vanishing act."

He paused and gave the audience a long look. "...Now I ask you, does this sound like a story we'd run here on Focus America? A mysterious avenger? An un-caped crusader? On our Program? To quote an American Icon named John Wayne, 'Not Hardly!'

"While I worked here on a story for an upcoming edition of Focus America I started collecting bits and pieces of this new legend like I once did in Minnesota about Paul Bunyon. I thought I'd file a gag story when I got home. It would be good for a few grins around the office. That's when the legend of The Blaster landed right in my lap." Fade out.

Fade in to an exterior day shot. Camera zooms into the building's entrance. Interior shot: "This is the Night Owl Cafe in the Jenkins Building. There are investment firms and other businesses here that are staffed twenty-four hours a day. The Cafe never closes. I had arranged to meet a source here for a pre-interview conference. Julie Gordon, my producer came with me. Late in the evening, we finished our business and the source departed.

Now Van Loan stands by a booth inside the Cafe. "Julie and I sipped coffee and went over our notes. A few couples and singles occupied scattered seats. Over there sat a party of five very well dressed men..."

"What you will see now are black and white stills taken by a security camera out in the building lobby. We've enlarged and computer enhanced them.

"Some dust fell into my coffee. I looked up and saw a panel of the drop ceiling pulled back from within." Cut to shot of black hole in the ceiling, then back to the grainy stills. "Before I could even start to speak to Julie, a black form dropped out of the hole and landed lightly on the bench seat beside me. He hopped over the table and dashed swiftly toward the group of five. Before he reached that area, four of the men drew hand guns. I heard the hammers fall. Nothing happened. Before the gunmen could recover form the shock of all of their weapons misfiring, the man in black waded in to them. In what looked like a bad fight scene in a low budget movie, he sent the two on the aisle sprawling. He grabbed the table and yanked it out amid flying dishes. He smashed a third gunman into the forth, then rabbit punched them out of the picture. He glanced around to assure himself that the first two gunmen stayed down."

Van Loan now stands next to the scene of the action. "By now I was telling myself that the mysterious Blaster lived only in local beer stories. He couldn't be real."

The stills again. They resemble extra slow Anime cartoon action. "The fifth member of the group stood up. The masked figure placed a hand on his shoulder and he sat back down. The man pointed to his chest and the fifth man relaxed a little. I couldn't see anything, but the camera caught it." Cut to an even grainier close up of the figure's torso. "In all the other stills, his black shirt seemed blank. When he pointed at it, ...a mark or logo appeared. Glowed, said some who had a clear view of it. The man in black knelt and rammed his hand through the front side of the u-shaped bench seat. The hand cut along the length of the seat like a hot knife through butter. He then yanked the cushion up. Reaching in, he removed a shoebox sized package. What he took from the box sent my head spinning."

"I spent three years as an Army Combat Engineer. I know a

demolitions device, or bomb, when I see one. There appeared to be enough plastic explosive in the device to destroy the restaurant and perhaps render the whole building unsafe. Speaking of unsafe, what he did next would be suicide for you or me.

"I'll use this copy to show you. The man in black simply yanked out the blasting cap without regard to possible booby traps. He held the wires leading to the explosive cap in his left hand. He scooped up a cloth napkin and took the cap itself in his right. For no apparent reason, the wires parted between his fingers and the cap came free. He then placed the normally very dangerous blasting cap on one of the scattered coffee saucers. Quickly he collected all four handguns. He removed single cartridges from three automatics and two from the sole revolver. These he also put on a saucer. Before he finished collecting the shells, smoke and sparks began pouring from the blasting cap. He glanced over briefly. No hint of expression showed on his goggled face. He turned and waived his hand over the plate with the mis-fired rounds. In seconds, they turned bright red. I could feel radiated heat on my face.

"I looked up at the mystery man. When I glanced back at the shells they had begun to lose their shape. When I looked up again, the man in black had already passed through the Night Owl's door. Another security camera recorded his dash to a side exit. He appeared to be loping easily along. Later I checked the timing of the camera frames against the distance he covered. At that rate, our mysterious friend broke ten seconds for one hundred meters.

"There is a mystery in this town. The Blaster, so named after he appeared to blast all four wheels off of a drive-by-shooter's car, seems to be a master of explosions without apparent explosives. You have just seen the only known pictures of him. If I had not been in the Night Owl Cafe when they were taken, I would not have filed this story. But I was there... I saw... I intend to find out more. This is Curtis Van Loan for Focus America..."

Much later that evening I climbed the back fire-stairs to my third floor loft. My mind kept running back and forth between Van Loan's report and the many conversations I'd participated in afterwords. Up until today the Blaster simply did not exist to most cops. Many who had seen him kept quiet about it. Afraid they'd get sent to the Department Shrink if they repeated what they'd seen. I was still enough of a Cop that I heard most of the locker room talk about the Blaster. What the senior brass knew, or believed, no one could say. Officially he simply did not exist.

Now there were pictures, of something, someone. One recurring scene at Silos began with the whispered words: "So you thought I was crazy…"

The brass would have to take some sort of position, I decided. I ran my key through both deadbolt locks and opened the door. The night light shone in the studio area. It felt good to be back among my projects in work. I looked each one over as I do every time I enter this way. Each setup contained a notebook ready for me to write down any new data, or flash of insight as I passed. I felt comforted seeing what my hands created, but the news report still held too much of my attention.

Light drifted in from my living quarters. I started to leave the studio area when it hit me. That was not my just my automatic night light. I had not needed to turn any lights on that afternoon to program the VCR's. I hadn't left the TV on, either.

I angled away to the electrical breaker box on the studio wall. Once there I knelt and pulled the small automatic pistol from my ankle holster. As I rose I took a five D-cell solid aluminum flashlight from its rack on the wall. A coil of rope hangs next to the flashlight. I took it and made sure that the line slid freely through the eye-bolt in the brick wall.

I payed out the line as I moved toward my living area. A series of moveable partitions separate the two areas. I peeked through a couple of cracks and located someone sitting on my couch watching the late news on the N-Cubed affiliate.

I tiptoed down to a corner where two partitions met. I took the flashlight and the lanyard in one hand, with the gun in the other. I braced my left foot and put my right one against one partition which just happened to be on rollers. I checked the line for tautness, then yanked.

The other end of the line threw the main circuit breaker. All light vanished. I shoved the partition aside and stepped through and to the side. Holding the flashlight in the old FBI style, at arm's length, I threw the high powered beam at the couch. "Stay where you are. I'm a Police Officer and I'm armed."

The figure had not moved. Slowly he placed his arms in full view on the back of the couch. When he spoke the voice seemed familiar.

"Of course you are armed Bowen Chadwick. Such a fine Celtic name. Bowen, Son of Owen. Chadwick, the Protector. Very appropriate, even to a Dutchman like me. We have to talk, my friend… About the Blaster."

Slowly, arms still extended, he rose and turned to face me. I'm glad the only light in the loft shone in his eyes. My face must have been something to see when I recognized Curtis Van Loan.

Chapter 2

# Into The Darkness... Again

As the plane took off I couldn't believe myself. Less than two hours ago I'd come home to find TV reporter Curt Van Loan sitting on my couch watching his network station on my set. But I'd never met the man. Now, wearing a disguise he'd provided, I sat strapped into the seat of a private jet clawing for altitude at about three G's. Under my seat lay a bag of gear I never intended to let anybody see. I went back over the scene in my loft apartment and studio. He'd just told me we needed to talk about The Blaster.

Van Loan stood still as I checked out the rest of the loft. He kept a look on his face that I couldn't quite figure. He appeared totally relaxed, but I could almost feel some sort of underlying tension. I patted him down. I found no weapons, but several very up to date electronic gadgets.

Finally I faced him across the living area. "Now, Mr. Mild-Mannered Reporter, you said we needed to talk. You can start by convincing me why I shouldn't just call the precinct and ask them to come and pick up the intruder I discovered."

"Because you care about people and I need your help to potentially save hundreds of lives. I'd planned on meeting you socially before I confronted you, but there's no time for that now. The Blaster's abilities could prevent a major tragedy. Therefore I need you."

To say that Van Loan set my mind spinning understates the issue exponentially. I took a deep breath, tried to keep my face from moving, and chuckled. "The Blaster? He's supposed to be all smoke and mirrors. What would I know..."

"Chadwick, give me some credit. I followed you to Silos tonight. I left as soon as you had the bartender change the TV to N-Cubed. I know you saw my piece on The Blaster. Then I came here. Ever since the incident in the Night Owl Cafe I've dug into every aspect of the Blaster's activities. You're still new at the double identity game. The Blaster has made some mistakes. Not big ones. Not ones that can't be buried by The Blaster's future activities. When I put all my data together a 98%

probability exists. Either The Blaster lives in a cave and you give him assignments somehow, or you are The Blaster."

Suddenly I started to worry. "Me, The Blaster? With my schedule? You're joking."

"Like I said, beginner's mistakes. I took every appearance of The Blaster, even the rumors, and analyzed them. His story got started by his middle of the night roller-blading through the worst parts of town. He began with targets of opportunity. Crime he couldn't turn his back on. Protecting people caught in the middle. Then came the Henderson kidnapping. The first time The Blaster actually tried to break a major crime. Other cases followed. I built a list of everybody even remotely connected to each case. Guess what? One way or another you show up on every one of them. So did two or three others, but I soon managed to place all of them somewhere else during a Blaster appearance. Every time The Blaster has caught a fugitive, freed a hostage, or recovered missing property Bowen Chadwick has some minor connection.

"Remember I got an close up and personal view of The Blaster at the Night Owl. You really ought to pad that black outfit some more. Once your name came up I watched you closely. You have the right body. Seeing you and some of your buddies shooting hoops and playing volleyball told me you had some of the same moves. Spending several hours in this loft tells me where I should be able to find all the proof I need. I'm pretty sure I know how you come and go privately. With a crowbar I'd collect most or all of The Blaster's gear in five minutes. The Blaster's new at this. I'm not."

The plane reached cruising altitude. As the pressure eased up on my body I felt more relief than just from the strain of acceleration. I knew I'd done the right thing. I've always had good instincts on who to trust and not to trust. They served me well when I was a full time cop. Served me well during my long hospitalization. Still serve me well. We'd sparred a bit longer, but I knew somehow that Van Loan meant every word he said. Then he clinched it.

"Chadwick, like I said, The Blaster may be new to this. My family's been involved with people like him for over one hundred and fifty years. Independent Operators we call them. Most of them don't wear masks, but some do. Almost since the first corruption showed up in the first civilization, the Independent Operator emerged to try and put things right. The Havens and Van Loans have been supporting them. Sometimes being them, since before the Civil War.

"The Blaster is not alone, but Heavens International Media does all it can to keep I.O. profiles low. I put that story on tonight for two reasons. One to get your attention for this meeting. But more importantly I put a big 'is-this-a-hoax' spin on the piece. Focus America is a trusted source. Now, if a certain tabloid TV show goes ahead with the full show expose they're planning, I've laid as many honest seeds of doubt as I can.

"I know most of the active Independent Operators in this country. Some only as a news source, but a few a lot better. The Voice, one of the best, (We played together as kids.) called me for help. He's deep undercover with a Right-Wing hate group. The Blaster's abilities may be the only thing that keeps Timothy McVey and Oklahoma City from being the first of many similar attacks."

Five minutes later we headed for the former Naval Air Station where the jet waited.

I'd been pretty tired when I'd entered my loft. Been awake for thirty-six hours. Now I had a short time to get rested. I started the meditation routine I'd learned from that Indian orderly at the hospital. Breathe. Let your mind concentrate only on the act of breathing. Repeat and concentrate. After just two minutes of this I'd shut out the noise of the jet. Cut out the vibrations. Lost the idea that Van Loan sat across from me. Cut off everything but me breathing. Then I let go and felt myself falling into the dark cavern of sleep.

Directed sleep often carries a price. You relive what's foremost in your mind. I stopped falling. Light returned to a small extent. I sat in the patrol car with Terry Faulkner rolling on a silent alarm call. We'd just pulled up to Quantum-Tek Laboratories. Disaster lay ahead, but we had no clue. We headed for the guard shack.

Terry and I approached the two inch thick window that let people talk to the security staff. I knew the design of the guardhouse. Two rooms and three doors,with one door to the outside of the fence. One door to the inside of the fence, and one between the rooms. Like an airlock on a space ship, only one door could be open at a time. A uniformed security guard appeared behind the glass. He greeted us almost too cordially.

I let Terry explain about the report of a silent alarm inside while I looked around. Most people would not have noticed several of the security features I saw. The place reportedly contained an Internet start-up company that spent big bucks putting this large compound together to have room to expand. The decorative planters and sculpture pylons just happened to form a perfect vehicle barrier. Various things, flush with the pavement could pop up and trap or disable anything this side of a Bradley Fighting Vehicle. All this for a bunch of servers and sales people?

I felt uneasy. The guard laughed off the alarm. Problems were common as new space got converted, he told us. Terry called back in, but the alarm had not been cleared through proper procedure. Finally I took over from Terry and insisted that he let us in for a look around, or connect us with his supervisor.

He hesitated, but finally opened the outer door for us. Terry went in first. I used the cover his body gave me to pull out my two handled night stick. I held the short handle with the long stick along my forearm. Something didn't feel right. I stepped into the very dark room and let the door close behind me.

As the door clicked shut they jumped us. One black clad figure came from behind the door. Another emerged from a pool of darkness to join the security guard in moving in on us. My instincts had been right. As soon as I felt the movement behind the door I pushed Terry forward with a yell. He went past the open mouthed guard before he or the other could react. At the same time I swept my arm up and back as I ducked low. Something whistled past my head. Charging from behind the door, the figure impaled himself on the end of my night stick just below the sternum. I drew my Glock service weapon as I rolled to the side.

Terry meantime spun around with his weapon in one hand and heavy flashlight in the other. The beam fell on the two figures he'd passed. From the floor I yelled, "Freeze! Twitch and I fire. Terry, check the room."

Terry quickly swung the light around the room. Only the three of them. The one behind me still tried to catch his breath. I kept the standing two covered while Terry cuffed them. The third guy stopped gasping as Terry used disposable plastic cuffs on him.

None of them said a word in answer to our questions. We used our last riot cuffs to lash their legs together then went through to the other room and outside. We left a chair blocking the outside door, effectively locking the three in the one room. I called the precinct for backup. Then we went scouting.

Terry and I circled the headquarters building. We saw nothing to indicate a break in. Using the shadows available we crossed to the next structure. This one had loading docks along the side and a number of connectors like the fire department uses to attach pumper trucks to a building's fire system. Six were right next to each other. That didn't make sense. I shielded my pen-light for a look. The hookups were made of at least three different materials.

Meantime Terry looked around the corner. He waived frantically. When I looked around I saw an open door about halfway along the rear wall. Standing next to it was a large figure in an overcoat.

Terry led the way. That side of the building was darker than a drug dealer's heart. Carefully we approached. We made no sound. Twenty yards from the look-out fate did us in. Two hundred yards away, and outside the compound fence, a car turned at corner. His high-beams washed over us when the perp happened to be looking in our direction.

Seeing two uniformed policemen with drawn weapons he yelled "Cops!" as he dived off the other side of the small raised concrete stair and slab. We heard him trip over something, but keep running.

"Guard the door," growled Terry, "I'll get him."

A moment later I looked inside through the bottom left corner of the open door. Some light spilled out from around what seemed to be a freestanding wall. It seemed bright as day inside, but every exterior window, and there were a lot of them, let nothing through.

Then I did something stupid. I decided to take a look inside.

I slipped up to the wall blocking the outside view. I looked around the end of it. Don't remember what I expected to see, but behind that wall didn't even come close. The four story building seemed to have been hollowed out. All that remained of the upper floors looked like viewing galleries that extended a few yards from the walls. Filling most of the ground floor, and, I assumed, any basement was an Olympic sized pool. No make that an Olympic sized vat made out of Lexan, or Lucite, about eighteen inches thick. The vat ended about twelve feet above floor level. A thick, viscus, transparent fluid filled the vat. It churned, as though stirred by some huge paddle. I could not see any device that might be causing the constant movement. The light began to hurt my eyes. I pulled my polarized sunglasses from the case on my belt. With the glare reduced I could see through to the far side of the vat. Behind the other transparent wall three men unhurriedly packed files and computer tapes into knapsacks. The humming inside the room had kept them from hearing the guard's warning. They concentrated on the task at hand with no apparent thought of interruption.

Believing I could get the drop on them, I started around the huge vat. My vague shadow followed me, always being on the wall to my left. That's when I realized that all the light in the room came from the liquid itself. I passed the four steps to a small platform surrounded on three sides by what looked like solid Sapphire. The bright glow barely penetrated the thick material. At the vat's corner I noticed a large pipe dispensing a thin stream of purple liquid into the thicker than molasses substance filling the thing.

I came around the corner at just the wrong time. One of the three put down a full knapsack and reached for another one. Even at fifty yards away I saw his mouth form the word "Cop!" He yanked a .44 Magnum out of his coat. I dived back around the corner of the vat. The pistol boomed. Chips from the concrete floor showered me. As he aimed again one of his companions tried to grab his arm. The second bullet smashed a metal box that sat over that big pipe.

Suddenly the purple liquid sprayed all over the vat like an oil gusher. The level of light rose exponentially. My skin began to prickle, even under my uniform. I ran for the door. A huge tendril of the thick liquid flowed over the wall ahead of me. By the time I stopped, it lay in my path two feet tall with no apparent inclination to flow any further. A similar amount rose from the vat above me. I jumped back as the level of light increased still more.

Then I noticed that platform just ahead of me. I flew up the steps. With my back to the four inch thick material I hunched down in the fetal position with both arms covering my eyes. A few seconds later I saw a flash of light that reached my retinas through the back of my head. As the light faded out, so did I.

Todd Browning and his partner Georgia Granger later told me what happened outside. They rolled to a stop behind our empty cruiser at the Quantum-Tek gate. They got out and looked around. As expected, the gatehouse door was secure and nobody answered the intercom. A third vehicle carrying the Sergeant of the Watch rolled up. Sampson Jones unfolded himself from behind the wheel.

"Find anything?" came his rumble.

"Quiet as a tomb," replied Granger

At that moment all three felt a brief vibration through their shoes.

"That happen before?"

"No, Sarge," said Browning. "No movement. No sound. Nothing. At least before you arrived."

A third unit pulled up. "Check the back line," Sam told them.

They said that Sam then walked over the gatehouse to try the intercom. He pushed the button just as the brightest light any of them had ever seen erupted from the building on the left side of the entry drive.

From Sam I learned that at least four layers of heavily smoked glass protected his eyes to an extent. Seemingly solid bars of hideously greenish light shot out of any number of windows in the building. Sam ducked behind the solid gatehouse door shouting "Down!" to the others. Through the now seemingly transparent gatehouse glass he could make out our three suspects bound on the floor. Closing his eyes, he began a count in his head, "One-Chimpanzee Two-Chimpanzee Three-Chimpanzee" At ten seconds the light no longer hurt his eyes through both his closed eyelids and the palm of his hand covering them.

Chapter 3

**Born... From The Darkness**

Van Loan's jet landed on a bumpy old air strip in the middle of nowhere. A stretch cab dually pickup truck with lots of red neck bumper stickers waited for us.

"Get more rest, if you can," he told me as he drove off.

The poorly sprung truck on those back roads turned out to be much harder to lose than the roaring jet. Finally I managed. The directed sleep dumped me right back into that crazy night.

I vaguely remember waking up in a smog thicker than the exhaust of a Greyhound bus. Maybe I thought it was smoke. I tried to crawl out. I went down the four steps head over heels. Right into a thick layer of goo.

Somehow I managed to turn over, then stand up. Guided by who-knows-what, I stumbled into the arms of the first fire fighters to reach that side of the building. Covered with goo, I slid right out of their grasp. Or so they told me later. I'd passed out.

When I woke up I discovered I lay on a table. I couldn't see well because some of that goopy stuff still clung around my eyes. I began to hear a myriad of sounds around me. I thought I could make out Sam Jones' voice cutting through the garbled noise. Had a preacher at my home church now and then with a voice like Sam. Never seemed to raise the volume, but could he ever project. Any sentence with an exclamation point and all the church windows rattled.

I tried to raise my head and look around. A gloved hand gently, but firmly brought it back down. A shadow fell across my eyes. I looked up to find someone in a HazMat suit with some kind of hose in his/her/its hand. From behind the respirator I barely made out the words, "Lie back, Patrolman. We're trying to get this stuff off of you." With that he placed the end of the hose, complete with a razor-like device somewhere around my navel and returned to shaving my bare chest.

Our Fire Department's HazMat folks keep earning an excellent reputation everywhere they go. I knew I was in capable hands. Before I lay back and relaxed I managed to croak out, "Faulkner.. Terry Faulkner, my partner?"

"We've seen him. He collared his suspect on the other side of the grounds. He just breathed in a little of the fumes trying to get to you. Medics will keep an eye on him. Once he changed out of his uniform he started helping at the Command Post. Just let go and relax. We'll do everything we can for you."

I let my eyes wander then. Finally I pieced together that I'd had a transparent plastic bubble put up around me. Sam, as Sergeant of the Watch, stood just outside the Command van nearby. Lieutenants, Captains, and others would arrive soon. Sam stood where he could hear the traffic in the van while he worked his uniform radio, and a cell phone. A long line ran from a headset around his neck back into the van. Someone dressed in full S.W.A.T. gear stood beside him. I faded away for a little while.

The poking and prodding necessary to attach a large set of vital sign monitors dragged me back to the light. I guess by then they'd shaved every hair on my body. A 'space-blanket' kept me warm. Near silence replaced the clatter and chatter outside the bubble.

I looked over at Sam just as his cell phone rang. "Sheffield!" his voice boomed. "Do you have any idea how busy I am? You've been what!? They are? Misbegotten… Badge Happy! Thanks, Sheffield. I owe you. And I know you'll collect."

Still in a semi-fog I vaguely remembered a reporter named Sheffield. I watched Samson Jones take a few deep breaths and slowly bring his hands together as if in prayer. I'd only seen that a couple of times. The old Viking tradition of the Berserker warrior gives us our word berserk. Out of control. Sam Jones at the absolute end of his patience in a crisis becomes intellectually berserk. And God help any soul who crosses him.

"Mendoza!" If Mendoza, the S.W.A.T. team leader, lay sound asleep at home he'd have responded. "Mendoza, I just got word that the Feds are working on a court order to take this crime scene away from us and confiscate any samples and evidence that could help treat our people. Get your welding gear, chains and the heaviest padlocks available. I want every possible way into this compound sealed tight. To include storm sewers. Move it. In the van, did you hear that? Good! Call the senior people on the way here. Cell phone only! Divert them to behind the Wall-Mart four blocks over. Then stand by for a fax. Public Affairs, listen up! Bring the reporters up to the section of the fence closest to this van."

With that he pulled out his cell phone. The last thing I heard as I faded out again: "Mrs. Nordquist? Good evening. Samson Jones here. Is His Honor in? Yes, I'm afraid it is urgent..."

When my mind stumbled back into the light things looked different, somehow. A makeshift screen lay between me and the section of fence where I knew half the reporters in town now lurked. The noise that roused me repeated itself. Heavily distorted laughter from under the hoods of three HazMat suits. I raised my head to look. A pair of hands lightly gripped my temples and cheekbones. Instead of pushing me back down, the hands pointed me towards a surreal scene.

The Quantum-Tek facility parameter kept visitors out with an impressive metal fence made to look like a phalanx of spears. Only instead of a single row of points there were four rows. Under a coat of paint those things were pretty sharp. Someone in the dark suit of a Federal Agent tried to climb over those points from the roof of a sedan that was not quite tall enough. First his pants leg got caught. Then he got jabbed in the thigh. Finally he dropped free on the inside. Only the last inch of his cuff snagged something as he let go. He did a full somersault and landed on his feet like a cat. I thought I heard a smattering of applause.

I watched as he schooled his expression back to all business. He walked purposefully towards the Command van. Sam wrote on a clipboard as he approached, appearing not to know he had company. I knew better. Any clipboard Samson Jones might carry reflects light better than most mirrors. Sam was ready. He and the Fed exchanged a couple of sentences that I couldn't hear. The the rubber met the road.

"Special Agent Simmons," rumbled Sam, "someone has been operating an unlicensed chemical plant on this site. That illegal operation, by unfortunate circumstances has killed three men believed to be committing a crime or crimes on the premises. Therefore this property is both an emergency toxic waste cleanup site and a municipal and state crime scene. Unless the unidentified bodies are federal employees acting with proper search warrants, there is no federal crime here."

The Fed said something to low for me to hear. I could feel Sam's reply wash over me. The Fed cringed at the intensity.

"Special Agent, I do not care if the ghost of J. Edgar Hoover himself comes up to me with a request signed by the ghosts of Elliot Ness, Wyatt Earp, and Sherlock Holmes, I will not relinquish control of this environmental travesty. That is until you prove to me that the people running this facility are agents of a foreign power engaged in crimes against this nation. Conversely, if you prove to me that this is a clandestine federal operation I will arrest the entire staff for violating statutes of this city, this county, and this state. And possibly you, for aiding and abetting."

To myself I quietly said, "Go get 'em, Sam!"

"Sergeant Jones, that gives me no choice but to serve you with this order from the Federal Circuit Court for this state. This orders you to vacate the scene immediately and hand over all materials in your possession."

Sam took the folded paper, glanced at it and put it under the clamp of his clipboard. He called over his shoulder at the van. "Detective Winslow, is it ready? Good! Bring it out."

Out of the van marched Dapper Dan Winslow in one of his signature tailored three piece suits. He carried a clipboard like a serving tray. This he handed to Sam with the flourish of a footman presenting a letter from the Queen.

"Simmons," Sam rumbled, probably rattling all the coffee cups in the van, "this is an order from Judge Nordquist of the Federal Court of Appeals for this state. He places this site in the hands of our city's Fire Department so that they may proceed with containment of the toxic spill and enjoins you from interfering in any way until such time as the Environmental Protection Agency shall prove to him that this site is again safe.

"Now, if you want to escalate this urinating contest, be my guest. We have several extra HazMat suits available. Your team may borrow them and help us access the situation inside. Should you decline to help us out and share whatever information you have, I must ask you to leave. Our Public Affairs specialist is now soliciting volunteers to be pool reporters who will wear those same suits while touring the entire facility using our special cameras to transmit what they see to the TV trucks."

As I faded out one last time I knew Sam had won.


I spent the next nine months in various medical facilities. All of them were reasonably local. But it took the combined efforts of the Police Department, the police union, the local media, and Sampson Jones' incredible list of connections, to keep the Feds from spiriting me away to some super-secret location.

At first totally without energy, I practically vegetated. Every time I tried to get out of bed I'd encounter a Fed with questions or medical test gear. Slowly energy returned. Boredom set in. Then the doctors, the ones who didn't see me as just a lab rat, became worried I wasn't sleeping enough. The more energy I regained, the less sleep I seemed to need. Three to four hours and I felt ready for another day. That just couldn't be enough, said the doctors. That started pills, then injections. And another legal brawl.

Just how Sam met Judge Nordquist I never found out. I got to know him pretty well. Quite a bit of new patient's rights legal precedents came out of my case. After he quashed an attempt to get me declared incompetent to make my own treatment decisions the craziness mostly stopped. But watching continued. I began pretending to sleep longer. With instrumentation banned I read books in the john at night. Then I discovered a covert way out of my room through the drop ceiling. From there I managed to get into the room where training aids were stored. I watched recordings of anything that remotely interested me. The biggest thing turned out to be a nearly one-thousand hour American Sign Language course. Before I left the hospital I watched it twice. And did all the exercises. That, and prerecorded movies kept the long nights full.

I spent the days trying to get released. When my latest ploy failed I'd head to the Activities Department for long term patients. I've always been a bit of an artist. Now I put all those high school classes to work. As my energy ever so slowly increased, I moved from pencil sketches, to watercolors, to acrylics, then on to clay sculpture. And I loved every minute of it.


Van Loan's voice broke me out of my flickering dreams as the truck approached a beat up wide spot in the bad Georgia road. Not even the birds seemed awake yet as the vehicle pulled into repair area of an old filling station. In fact, the building probably started out as a livery stable.

A nondescript man in mechanics coveralls sealed the swinging wooden doors behind us. He and Van Loan exchanged seemingly casual greetings. But I felt a large amount of energy between them as they spoke. Not to mention I could feel two handguns well concealed on the mechanic.

He walked over to a workbench to switch on a radio. Suddenly Johnny Cash filled the building getting that car *One Piece At A Time*. Then he led us to the shop office and closed the door.

Johnny Cash stayed mostly outside. Van Loan pulled out what looked like a Walkman unit. He waved it around, then returned it to his pocket.

"You think I missed something, Curt?"

"Just being thorough," replied Van Loan with a light chuckle sticking out his hand. "How ya' been, pal?"

The handshake turned into a quick session of mutual back slapping.

"'Bout as well as this business gets, old friend. Speaking of friends. Is this him?"

Suddenly all business, Van Loan said, "That's right. He's agreed to come in. Blaster, meet The Voice."

This was the top Independent Operator? His face seemed so ordinary I'd have trouble sketching it in person. Much less from memory. But then, few people but me would have realized he was armed. He turned to the side briefly. He cleared his throat with a hand on his Adam's Apple area.

"Pleased to meet you!"

Dear God! I couldn't believe my ears. I understood every word perfectly, but the sound. The sound. Every word seemed to be spoken by a different person. Actually, the world "pleased" changed tone and pitch three times!

I tried to keep my face still. Didn't work. Curt Van Loan broke out laughing. A restrained chuckle came from the Voice. That sounded even weirder than his speech. The two looked at each other with big grins.

"Sorry, friend," said Van Loan, getting himself under control. "It's always an adventure seeing somebody's first reaction to his signature sounds."

I think I smiled a bit before saying, "Makes Alvin and the Chipmunks sound positively normal."

That brought another brief round of laughter. The Voice turned aside again with the same throat gesture.

"That's a comparison I've never heard before," he said in the same voice he used outside the room. "From what Curt says, you can control explosives. My case may involve them by the ton. How much can you handle? And how?"

Now this was a lecture I never expected to give. To anyone. I remembered my first discoveries involved anything but explosions. I'd rubbed my hands over a block of pink granite and one of marble to try to "feel" the shapes inside. Later I discovered the outer layer where I rubbed fell away to sand as I picked them up.

"I seem to have control of certain chemical bonds and reactions," I began as I picked up a clipboard from the desk. "Any secret writing on this top sheet?"

The Voice shook his head. I tore off the sheet of paper and wadded it up. I tossed it toward the high ceiling. A split second later confetti rained over all of us.

"I can feel explosive potential. This includes the compression cycle of most internal combustion engines. I can stall them. I can make them more efficient. Sort of like a turbo-charger. I can cause explosions in most non-explosive materials. Distance makes it tougher. Up to a point I can make explosives go off. I can also delay them from exploding. Also up to a point. I could set off a round in either of your weapons. Or all the rounds. If you tried to take a shot at me I could cause the primer not to ignite. That is until I left the area, or fell asleep.

"As for how much? I don't know. The biggest I ever did was lock down about ten kilos of C4. I had no trouble at all keeping it inert for the half an hour it took to get it into a sink hole outside of town. I dropped it in and walked away. A quarter mile and over a hill later it went off when I could no longer feel it. The best thing to do with a large amount is to block the blasting caps, or det cord, or whatever. Then remove and dispose of them before they can enable the main charge. That help?"

"Gives me some ideas," he replied. "Curt sent me his N-Cubed piece and the stuff he didn't put in. Everything, but who he thought you were. If you don't mind, I'd like to see what you can do for myself. We're not expected back in the bad guy's compound until noon tomorrow."

Inside the gas station proper Van Loan and the Voice threw together a pretty decent breakfast as we waited for dawn. Then we headed out the back and down into a fairly deep ravine. For then next two hours we played normally dangerous games with various commercial and home brewed explosives and munitions.

Back in that office other country singers muffled our

conversation. Then the Voice got down to business.

"Organizations of the far American Right Wing have mostly been splintered for the last couple of generations. Since the murder of American Nazi Party founder George Lincoln Rockwell the few attempts at unification, or even cooperation, have been almost laughable. Thank heavens. But a few years ago I took down an organization out of Colorado. In their papers were links to other groups. Most were small outfits built around a charismatic leader. But someone, somehow, managed to get them to cooperate on various 'common good' projects.

"In fact, this Coordinator, as he's known, seemed about ready to propose a national right wing action plan. Oklahoma City changed that. Even groups who would have applauded the bombing of a strictly FBI facility were appalled. Now the Coordinator has only the most virulent hate, isolationist, and revolutionary groups listening. He's been whipping them up as much as he can from the shadows.

"Curt and I began picking up intel of something big. Intel from some of the less violent hate groups, even. That intel pointed to the Chattahoochee Militia here in Georgia. They've called in every favor they've even been owed, and then some. All for some top secret 'project.' The Militia is as isolationist as they come. They hate foreigners. They think America should mine both the Mexican and the Canadian borders. Then shut down all sea ports. Then tell the rest of the world to leave us be, or get nuked.

"A few months back, one of the Coordinator's smaller groups got busted up near my hometown. Several died in a shootout. I took over the identity of one of their members. I drifted this way making contacts as I went. The Militia finally took me in. I don't know what they plan, but its big. And its soon. And it involves explosives. A couple weeks ago I 'discovered' that one of my buddies escaped death or capture. That's you."

I thought for a moment, then asked, "Just how far inside are you?"

"Only far enough that they can slam the door and all my work will be legally useless. Not even enough to talk a drunken judge into any kind of search warrant. They send me on errands. A lot of them have been put-ups to test me. I even hoe their blessed vegetable garden."

He paused a moment shaking his head. Then, "After a couple belts of moonshine, Poppa Adams, their leader, told me that once the current operation is over I'll be in so deep I couldn't turn them in, if I wanted to. If it wasn't for the women and children in the compound, I'd be sorely tempted to use my honorary Uncle Dick's scorched earth methods. Go Mack Bolan on 'em. Damn! I'm flat frustrated."

Van Loan broke the silence that followed, "Let's get started on his face and prints."

The Voice snapped out of his funk with, "True enough. He's going to need the practice in character…"

I spent the next few hours in a bedroom above the gas station. Van Loan stripped off the facial disguise he'd helped me put on. "That's it for amateur night," he remarked. Was it ever.

First he gave me the closest shave of my life. Then he rubbed, painted, and troweled various concoctions on to my face, neck, and ears. He told me the treatment basically turned my pores as far off as possible and even retarded beard growth. Then he glued semi-soft appliances in various places to change the shape of my face.

The Voice took no part in this. He didn't need to see my real face. Didn't want to. Curt Van Loan knew me. That was enough. Once everything hardened came what Curt called the base-coat. He applied three extremely thin layers of something that ended up the consistency of human flesh. Once that set up he let me touch it. Darned if it didn't feel like caressing somebody else's face. Then he built a form around my face and created a 'life mask' of his work out of a very strange smelling goo.

Since I had to hold still for half an hour I managed to direct myself back into sleep.

This dream surprised me. Pleasantly. The winter I moved into my loft. I'd started to build a small reputation for painting and sculpting. The fact that I could sort of dissolve small amounts of stone and some metals helped a little with production times. This particular Sunday Sampson Jones hosted an all day Super Bowl party. I'd agreed to come early and paint the team mascots on half sheets of Bakelite for decoration. But the city got hit by an overnight ice storm.

Jones' place lacked just a bit of being two miles from mine. With a knapsack of paints and brushes on my back I slipped out the side door of the building. Behind a high privacy fence the sidewalk to the parking area shimmered in the now cloudless skies. Slicker than snake-snot, I remember thinking. I got about half way along it when the back pack shifted!

I skimmed down the sidewalk. I felt my feet start to go out from under me. I threw out my arms, trying to reach a wall. Suddenly I found myself still and fully upright. But my hands had touched nothing!

In fact, I was facing the building wall, but my hands seemed to be pushing off something. Empty air, as it turned out. I tried to take a step. Again I started to slip. I raised my left arm and pushed. I slid ten feet down the sidewalk. Then my right arm brought me to a stop. Touching nothing.

On that sidewalk I spent the next five minutes convincing myself I wasn't dreaming. On the glaze ice I seemed to be self-propelled. Finally, I said to heck with the van. I turned around and basically ice skated to Sam's.

By spring I determined I could produce about one-hundred foot/pounds of thrust. By the fall, using roller-blades, I could out maneuver, sometimes out speed, just about anything on city streets. The blading helped me burn energy so I could sleep. And helped the Blaster come into being.

By the time Van Loan removed the life mask I was completely slept out. But the renewed light on my face hurt my eyes. I slid back down on the bed with an arm loosely thrown over them. A few seconds later the Voice entered.

"Is he asleep?" he signed to Van Loan.

Before Curt could answer I sat up and signed back, "Not asleep. My eyes hurt."

The Voice chuckled, "Now that's one skill you missed, Curt. Doesn't happen often. Your eyes will be fine, Blaster. Half an hour, or less. I don't even notice it anymore."

A touch red with embarrassment Van Loan asked, "American Sigh Language isn't in either of your profiles. How'd I miss that?"

"You know when I had all that spare time?" I asked with a smile I wasn't sure showed through the stuff on my real face. He nodded. "Two to five a.m. most nights watching tapes and practicing in front of a mirror. I've only used it a couple of times as the Blaster. My 'accent' must be positively wooden."

"Got a head's up for you," replied Van Loan with a smile. "That red-head you met last night? She's fluent in ASL. Thanks to one of her grandmothers being deaf."

"Red-head?" inquired the Voice.

Van Loan and I replied in unison, "Never mind!"

My undercover experience amounted to nil, or thereabouts.

Fortunately the Voice picked a dead easy and secretly dead character for me. Fergus Hampstead had been a quiet, almost surely, loner. As far as anyone could tell he served the defunct organization at about the level of spear carrier. Absolutely reliable with no imagination. Not too hard for the former cop whose undercover work amounted to trying to buy beer without getting carded.

About the time Fergus finished appearing on my face, in walked the Voice wearing a face I recognized. Sort of. Now I remembered the news story detailing the end of Fergus' group. Later I read a BOLO (Be On the Look Out) flier for the group's members not in handcuffs or body-bags. Charles (Charlie) Pervs seemed almost handsome. But the face attached to the Voice extruded the same bitter outlook as that flier. Not someone I wanted dealings with. The three of us spent the rest of the day getting me ready to become Fergus. A very long day.

Just before we left Van Loan approached me. "I understand you can mark and later detect objects you've touched."

My eyebrows shot up as far as my disguise let them. "How'd you figure that out?"

"Part of my basic research into the Blaster. You tend to easily find things that your other self has been around. I know you presented Sally Henderson with a sketch the week before she got snatched. After the story broke, our affiliate got reports of any number of Blaster sightings. You began one big circle of the metro area. Then suddenly you started an inward spiral. Near the center of that area all Hell broke loose. Girl rescued. Perps seriously trashed. Then, Hi-Yo Silver, away. Either you're extremely psychic, or you detected her."

The upshot being that Van Loan asked me to "charge" six small items. He told me, "Once I have a likely target, I'll leave an equipment cache in the area. Commo and gear for both of you. I've duplicated your work clothes except for the glowing mark on the chest."

# Chapter 4

## Not
## Let's ^ Have A Blast

About an hour before noon the Voice turned a battered Ford Ranger off a horrible dirt road onto an almost non-existent pair of ruts into the woods. He got out to somehow open a battered gate. A gate that reminded me of D-Day tank traps. As we slipped into the tree line he remarked, "About a mile further."

"I'm not surprised," I replied. "Can feel the place already."

He replied as an overblown hill character, "Ya can? Th' Bubba's got that much 'splosive?"

"A huge amount? No. But I can feel where they've set off small blasts all through here. Something must have leaked going out, too. There's an almost washed away line under the left tires. Past this little hill it feels like the whole place's coated in explosive dust. Not enough anywhere to be dangerous, but I can detect it."

"Will that keep you from finding their big stash?"

"Not a problem. Be like finding the Mormon Tabernacle Choir in full voice surrounded by people humming."

A moment later we topped the small hill and headed into the headquarters of the Chattahoochee Militia. After parking in a seemingly random spot, we approached what looked like a big porch sticking out of a hillside.

A middle-aged woman greeted us from behind a door at the back of the porch. She looked like something out of the nineteenth century in the calf length check dress. That is until I noticed the walkie-talkie clipped to her apron. That, and behind the door I felt the sawed-off shotgun she held.

She nodded curtly to the Voice, "Who'd this be, Charlie?"

"The fella I went looking for, Mrs. Adams. Fergus Hampstead from my old group."

"Welcome Fergus," she began, "but there's some strings attached to it. Still a couple on Charlie, tell the truth. You're on probation. The men'll fill you in on most of that. On my side of things, don't speak to the children. 'Cept to say hello, or ask for directions. And, you so much as look funny at any of the older girls… Well, before the men haul off your carcass off, I'll be slowly makin' a steer out of you. Understand?"

I didn't have to fake a gulp before I managed to say, "Yes, ma'am."

"Now that's out of the way." She smiled, "Come on in. The men are working. Should be here for lunch. Charlie, pour the coffee. I'll get you some fresh rolls and preserves to hold you over."

With that she led us into the spartan looking building that seemed to mostly be in the side of the hill. 'Earth sheltered' I think they call it these days. The huge kitchen and common room had big windows that looked out onto the "road" we'd come in on. Hinges the size of my wrist held two inch metal plates ready to swing down and cover them.

"Nice curtains," I drawled in the sarcastic tones Fergus used.

"The Militia uses that two inch stock quite a bit. Good home security," replied the Voice, also in character.

Mrs. Adams bustled back up just then with a tray heaped high with fluffy looking biscuits and three kinds of home canned preserves. "Don't fill up too much," she advised. "Fresh country ham and sweet potatoes for lunch."

We both gave our thank you's as she headed out the front door.

"Don't worry, too much," said the Voice. "I got the exact same welcome."

"Dead serious, wasn't she?" I replied.

"I've seen her catch, slaughter, and dress-out large hogs without any help."

That brought conversation to a halt. We dug into the fresh biscuits and excellent preserves.

After a couple minutes of silence I began to feel something. At first just a nagging itch, then tension began to build in my body. Finally I could feel a tiny spot below us. The spot enlarged, then seemed to spread. And grew in intensity. And spread some more. And grew. And spread. I placed my hands flat on the table, then tilted them this way and that.

"You all right, Fergus?" asked the Voice.

"Just the sugar rush from those Elderberry preserves," I managed to say in character. I pulled my hands back into my lap. Where no camera or watcher could possibly see I finger spelled, "Explosives being brewed. Directly below us. Like 50 lbs TNT so far. Growing fast."

When we finished our coffee the Voice showed me the path to the out building where I would bunk. By then the explosives under the hill felt lots bigger than the five-hundred pounds of TNT I once checked out. About the time the walking tour ended I felt the stuff start to shift. While we chatted with the man walking the parameter of the compound the whole mess began to recede. By the time we reentered the common room, the whole Militia was sitting down to lunch. Aside from a bunch of personal weapons, the only explosives I could feel seemed to be less than the size of my fist. Swept, I supposed, into a trash barrel below us.

I got introduced to all and sundry. They seemed almost jovial, even if a little wary of me. I got the impression some of the good ol' boys smirked at me. I caught guarded wisps of conversation about everything being about ready. Good thing Fergus was an introvert. I almost felt too nervous to speak.

After lunch I received the "official" tour of the compound. And what was off limits to guests such as Charlie and me. Only one place we did not go: the infirmary. The small cabin, for want of a better term, served as the living quarters for one man. Tad Fleming, one of the Militia's founders, they told me, suffered from Tuberculosis, the super-bug variety. Tad wore a mask when not eating. So did anybody who attended him. We didn't need his bugs and he couldn't stand getting any of ours, either. He waved feebly to us from his wheelchair at one point. We received his greetings by relay.

That afternoon I helped the Voice tend the extensive vegetable garden. Plus I learned a thing or two about chickens and hogs. After the huge evening meal talk stayed general, almost guarded. I felt tired enough to go to sleep with the sun.

The following morning Stoney Jackson, the number two man, sat down with us as we feasted on a substantial breakfast.

"You two'll make a run this morning. Down to the Waffle House this side of Columbus. Park. Get a cup of coffee. You'll be picked up."

Soon we drove away in a medium sized commercial truck that obviously once belonged to U-Haul. The springs sagged on the thing. The Voice said the wheel felt very sluggish.

Still worried about possible bugs, the Voice signed to me in the midst of driving, "Any bang here?"

I replied in ASL, "Nothing, except your pistol."

Frustration flashed across his false face as he signed, "What in the <expletive deleted> are we hauling?" I have no idea what he actually signed. That video course didn't cover swearing.

A couple of police cars passed us as they went about routine business. And we went by one on the shoulder, as the cop wrote a ticket. I felt the ammo in their small arms through the load as the vehicles passed.

Something seemed very dense in the back of our truck. Then an over tricked out, supercharged, jacked-up pickup roared around us. The window rack behind the driver held both a rifle and shotgun six inches above my eye level. Loaded. This time I felt virtually nothing between the shells and myself.

Shortly, as the road cut through a stretch of heavy woods, I signed, "You need to heed the call of nature. Make sure a heavy tree branch scrapes the upper side of the cargo carrier when you stop."

He gave me a puzzled look. Two minutes later the former U-Haul shook a large oak tree coming to a side of the road halt. With the Voice pretending to take care of business, I rested one foot on the passenger's seat while I jammed the other between the cab and the cargo box. In the shadow of the tree branch I dissolved the heads of two rivets in the sheet metal sides of the cargo box connecting to an upright member. Using a couple of sticks I forced open a narrow slit.

The translucent plastic in the top of the truck allowed me to see fairly well. I saw tightly packed wooden and heavy plastic boxes about two feet tall. Each group of boxes sat in heavy wood framing to prevent any possible motion. Finally my eyes adjusted enough to read a couple of labels.

Back on the road a moment later, the Voice signed, "Give!"

"We're hauling ball bearings," I replied. "Half inch and three-quarter inch ball bearings."

Eventually we parked the truck at the edge of the Waffle House lot facing the County Road we'd come in on. The Voice stood by while I seemingly worked out the kinks pushing against the restaurant sign. I breathed, "Ball bearings. All she could carry. The leaf springs are about read to snap. I can only think of one use for 'em."

He gave me a grim look as he hissed one word, "Shrapnel."

The Waffle House coffee's tasted like last night's pot.

Riding under the camper shell in the back of that pickup drove me nuts. The Voice and I sat at the front of the bed. Two of the Bubbas sat at the back of the bed watching us. A stack of simulated boxes blocked the only window. I'd long since lost my lock on the Militia compound. I could feel more and more engines around us. And no big rig ones for some time. Then I began to feel explosives far ahead of us. Ten minutes later I decided that the only place I ever felt more potential than this was the huge commercial explosives plant fifty miles outside my hometown. And not by much.

The truck slowed. Then began to creep forward like in bumper to bumper traffic. Cars now completely surrounded us. I concentrated on feeling the traffic. Finally I decided we moved in the middle of four or five lanes. We turned right into much thinner traffic. Then a shift in the various weapons in the cab caught my attention. My feelings expanded beyond the roadway. The distant explosive mass resolved into a few small arms just ahead. Plus three widely separated concentrations of multiple tons each!

I barely managed to control my reaction as the nearest passed almost close enough to touch. Ground zero. Had to be. I rose from my seat as far as the low roof allowed. I did a couple of stretches. With my back briefly to the Bubbas I finger spelled "Three huge booms here," to the Voice. Then, "We just passed one." Two minutes later we went through some kind of check-point. Almost immediately we hopped a curb and stopped.

The pickup stopped with the camper shell backed up almost to the open door of a large RV parked along with several others. As we alighted in the darkness we couldn't see anything but the sides of vehicles. The Militia men hurried us into that open door. "All the way back," we were told.

The RV was brimming with right wing pictures, plus fancy looking electronics. And weapons. And empty explosives containers. But no ammo. Not even a blasting cap.

I felt guns drawn behind us. Two words flashed into my mind: Fall Guys!

With both of us being lone wolf operators, it took Curt Van Loan to arrange some preset action signals. If apart, the ASL sign for "I love you" a/k/a the Devil's Horns meant "Fight NOW!" If next to each other one would tap the other twice. I swung my hand for the Voice's leg. Our knuckles rapped together. Twice!

I clamped down on every bullet in the area. That put the Voice two tenths of a second ahead of me. The five Militia men crowded around us. For openers, the Voice's heel slammed down on the arch of Little Sammy's foot. He carried that move on to body block Marty Jones over the RV's tiny dining table. Marty's Smith & Wesson .32 went flying. The Voice rebounded towards the character known only as Mort.

By that time I'd buried a two arm elbow jab into Lucas' flabby belly. His wad of Red Man chew passed over my my leaning head like a tennis serve. That left Hollis Morton, the body builder, untouched. Hollis back peddled, bringing his Police Special into firing position. He yanked the trigger.

Nothing happened. He tried again. By then I'd moved just inside his weapon. I swept the piece to the side with the move my martial arts instructor laughingly called "Wax off." With two finger joints folded in, my other hand struck for the solar plexus. And bounced off. A smile began to form on his lips. If my next move didn't finish him I'd be forced to blast his brain into strawberry jam. I used my right hand's bounce to force my left shoulder forward. A knife hand four finger strike slammed into his Adam's Apple. The pain glazed his eyes over. As he crumpled I spun around.

To find the Voice mopping up. The edge of his hand finished punching Little Sammy's ticket to dreamland. Mort's arm looked broken. In two places. Marty Smith moved in the wreckage of the table. A snap-kick and he moved no more.

The Voice turned to glance at Hollis. "Nice recovery," he remarked as he started patting down the Bubba's.

He looked up sharply as I replied, "It was that, or squirt his brain out his ears."

"I hadn't thought of that," he admitted. "Now let's see where we are."

With that he pulled the cord of the curtains covering the rear windows of the RV. As we looked over some sort of control console I could see our faces reflected in the windows. Both our eyes widened. I fought to keep my jaw from dropping. Beyond our reflected images, less a hundred yards to the north, stood the Atlanta Centennial Olympic Stadium. The opening ceremonies appeared to be in full swing.

The Voice hurried outside. A moment later the RV's internal generator cut out. Apparently there was no external electrical hook-up. A couple of battery powered lights came on. As I finished tying up the Militia men he stuck his head in the door.

"Let's go. I've disabled both the generator and power input."

Seconds later we took stock from the RV's roof. The vehicle sat almost across from the southern apex of the irregularly shaped stadium. About a thousand feet to our left lay the depression holding the north-south Interstate highways I-75 and I-85. Near the highway and slightly north I felt the first bomb like a throbbing toothache. About sixty degrees east of north and about half again the distance away lay the second device. Dimly by comparison, I felt the third on the far side of the stadium.

We hurried toward the closest truck bomb. We dodged over, under, and through a maze of parked vehicles. Halfway there, through the haze of tons of sudden death, I felt the sharp point of a different type of signal. One of Van Loan's beacons! I pulled the Voice behind an empty paddy wagon. A few words and he stayed on course for the device. I doglegged to just this side of the security fence. Moments later I popped the welds on the back of a medium trash dumpster. From a hidden compartment I drew a large backpack. Tied to grommets were an all black speed laced pair of my favorite roller-blades, and a skateboard rigged with a snowboard's foot binding.

Silent. Somehow those blades were virtually silent on the pavement. I dodged here and there to avoid people and security cameras. The truck bomb turned out to be behind a temporary billboard that mostly served to hide bare dirt and screen off the highway. My recent touch allowed me to glide up behind where the Voice crouched. I almost got brained with a tire iron for my trouble.

A moment later he told me, "I think there's somebody under the trailer."

"Correct," I replied in a harsh whisper. "Someone with two long magazines of about eighty rounds each. Probably two sets of forties taped together. Seven blasting caps in the trailer. Must be electrical. Can't feel any fuse or det-cord."

The Voice opened the backpack. Out came a set of belts, pouches, and holsters. These he strapped on with practiced ease. "Let's go," he said.

We zipped through the last section of parking lot with me towing him on the skateboard. He held my belt with one hand. With the other he somehow managed to find and pull on a baggy black sniper's veil from the backpack. As we stopped he handed me my helmet with mask and a small breathing device.

"My guess is that this guard bails out by going down to the Interstate just a bit before show time," breathed the Voice in my ear. "These clowns don't tend to be suicidal." Boy, was he ever wrong.

I headed for the back end of the big rig trailer. The Voice got between the Bubba and the Interstate. I clamped down on the seven blasting caps and and all the ammunition in the area. Then the Voice tossed a gas bomb under the truck. He'd told me that almost everybody exposed to that gas took a deep breath by reflex. The thing was not really a bomb, but a sphere that sprayed his knockout gas in all directions. I heard the sharp hissing spray and the pounding feet as the Voice charged in its path. That's when we found out just how wrong his hunches had been.

I felt the long magazines sprint away from the trailer. One round from the weapon tried to discharge, but with no noticeable effect. I felt the cartridge detach itself from the rest and fall to the ground. The man did not try to fire again. He headed back in the general direction of the phony control center. I felt his weapon leave my area of influence.

By that time I had dissolved the lock hasps on the back of the trailer. A booby trap in the door tried to detonate the entire load. But I already had the blasting caps under my control. I climbed over barrels, boxes, and bags full of the home brewed explosive. Thirty seconds later I held the seven caps as I jumped back to the ground. I closed the trailer doors. Then I grabbed that expended round and headed after the Voice.

I found him crouched over a manhole, trying to pick the tumblers of a locking lug device.

"That was Tad Fleming, of all people. The bastard slithered down this thing," he told me.

"He's making pretty good tracks down there," I replied. "He'll be at the second device in less than two minutes. He's going a lot faster than we could with all the clutter up here. Let me at the thing."

Standing on the metal cover, I put my thumbs on the twin key slots. Then I applied will-power, for want of any better term. With a dull thunk the locking lugs shot down into whatever lay below.

We climbed down to discover an eight foot diameter almost dry pipe that stretched in both directions. The Voice pulled the skateboard off his back. A second later we headed after Tad.

We sped down the dark tunnel blind except that I could still feel Tad's machine-pistol somewhere ahead. At first his own pounding footsteps must have drowned out our rolling approach. Suddenly I felt the pistol stop, then move to a higher level. Like a weapon drawn and aimed.

Next I made out some light ahead. The storm drain tightened its curve, then straightened out. Probably anybody but me would have died as Tad triggered the Mac-10.

Nothing happened, of course. We heard a curse just as we piled into him. A couple of seconds later the Voice shined the flashlight in Tad's face.

"He's doped to the gils."

"Course I am. Only got 'bout three weeks ta live. Use lots of meds to keep going. Wanted to go out with a bang on the third truck. Watch the foreign scum run towards me for safety. Die as they get what's comin' to 'em. Won't see it now, but we'll all hear it. I started the short countdown when I saw you open that truck."

We left Tad tied to one of the metal rungs of a ladder out of the tunnel.

A few minutes later, I cupped fourteen blasting caps, and that expended round, in my hands as we hurried back to the storm drain system. I could feel the burning within them. Back in the distance I felt the first truck. Now like a dull toothache. On the other side lay the third big rig trailer. There I felt a sharpness within. With an extra mental squeeze I put down the explosive handful. The Voice slipped the the manhole cover back on. Then we took off.

I could feel the vast potential energy of the second truck recede. Then came the dull snapping sound as what was left in the blasting caps detonated. I felt the Voice's grip on my belt tighten, then relax a bit. I concentrated on shoving us faster down the tunnel.

A moment later we came around the sharpest turn so far. The beam of Tad's flashlight barely registered a two inch upward ledge just ahead. Instinctively I jumped. My helmet scrapped along the top of the concrete curve of the tube as I grabbed the Voice's arms. I felt the skateboard smack into the concrete lip. The Voice sprawled into me, then managed grab me in a heavy bear hug. How I remained upright I'll never know. Somehow I brought us to a stop without damage.

We were close. With the Voice now clinging to my neck I glided at reduced speed to the next manhole. I blasted off the cover's locking flanges. Then I pushed it aside.

We were under a bus. A low-slung bus. I scrambled out of the manhole as the Voice told me to head for the third truck. I needed no urging. The thing was further away than I thought at the edge of a fenced off staging area.

A couple minutes later I saw the Voice vault the fence where I'd zapped the razor-wire. He ran to where I leaned against the trailer marked " Johnston Concessions - Back-up Equipment."

"Give me a moment to get the doors open," he panted as he raced up.

"No," I managed to gasp out. "I got here too late."

"Too late? You don't mean…"

"That's right. I couldn't get a lock on the blasting caps. Still too far away. As I came over the fence they went off. Since then I've been holding off the detonation of the whole truck load."

The Voice headed deeper into the parking lot looking for a tractor unit. I ripped out the various booby traps from the trailer's wheels, air-lines, and such. The next thing I knew, the Voice roared up in the cab of a big rig. The snarling beast sported CNN decals, of all things. I guided him as he backed into the hook-up with one hand. I devoted the other hand to locking down the explosion building inexorably in the trailer.

The Voice popped out of the cab. He made the rest of the hook-ups.

As I walked back with him as he un-chocked the wheels. I managed to say, "This truck's different. I tried to dissolve a hole in the bottom to let the unaffected material drain out. The bottom's lined with that two inch steel plate. So's the side away form the stadium. I think the stadium side's packed with ball bearings."

The Voice spat out three ugly words in a language I didn't recognize. He bit a forth word in half before continuing, "A giant Claymore mine... Got to be! That's why the other trucks were so far away from the stadium. Everybody who survived those blasts would evacuate in this direction. And the international athletes would be leading the pack. I knew I should have just wiped the Militia out!"

Then we raced to the cab of the truck. I reached for the driver's door handle when the Voice stopped me.

"Can you handle a big rig?"

"Well enough," I hissed as I felt pressure coming from all sides of me.

"Drive and and ride herd on seven tons of boom? I don't think so. I can already see the strain in your eyes. One missed gear. Or a fender bender, and you might lose it... Just long enough. Get in the passenger side. I'll drive."

As soon as I hit the seat, keeping the lid on got just a bit easier. I could feel where the seven blasting caps set off sections of the main charge. In spite of all my efforts I felt seven rough spheres of detonation getting bigger than softballs. Each one kept expanding. Eventually the rest of the barrels of home brewed explosive would would catch the chemical reaction. Not that I felt it, but surely there must already be heat and gasses released by the explosions in slow-mo. I tried to run through those breathing and concentration exercises. Only a little help. The expansion slowed, but not much.

As we headed for the service gate I pulled more gear out of Van Loan's backpack. Most of it quickly disappeared into the Voice's pockets. A stack of ID cards for both of us stayed on the seat between us. Then I found an Iridium satellite phone.

Within seconds the Voice punched up a connection. He gave what seemed like a codename and password. After a brief pause he launched into a concise situation report. He put down the phone as we pulled up to the locked gate.

The lone guard walked up to the cab. I guess he started to tell us he didn't have the key. The Voice popped open the cab door to spray him in the face with smoke from a strange looking hand weapon. The guard crumpled almost instantly. A moment later we rolled through the now open gate.

Soon we headed south on Pollard Boulevard SW for the I-85 on ramp. Now the Voice gave details about the two trucks and the RV into the phone. Just before I lost sight of the stadium I saw two inspiring things. First a group of shadowy figures, professionals by their movements, closed in on the first truck. From the other direction came a dancing flame. The Olympic Torch entered the grounds. As we crossed under the highways to the entrance ramp the Voice ended his call.

He punched numbers again. Without preamble he began, "Curt I hope you know a place south of Atlanta safe to detonate a big rig full of explosives!"

He listened for a moment, then glanced over at me. "Can't defuse it. According to our friend, its already in the process of going off! Double time it, friend."

With that he put down the phone. He blew lungs empty. With a deep breath he turned in my direction. "That ought to light a fire under him!"

I never knew if my weak smile in return actually appeared on my face. "I don't know how long I can hold this. How can he possibly…"

"He'll come up with something," replied the Voice firmly. "Curt's a Finder. That's his gift. I needed help. He found you before he knew I needed you. Chances are…"

The satellite phone rang. The Voice hardly said a word beyond "Got it" and "Understood," and finally "Thanks, buddy. That's another five pounds of sushi I owe you."

"He found something?" I asked.

"Old quarry. About twenty-five miles from here. We'll drive this thing down to the bottom. Curt's on with the National Guard to evacuate that area. He's also working on something to extract us."

I blinked, "How does a newsman get the Guard to listen that quick?"

"Curt knows everybody. And where the bodies are buried," chuckled the Voice. "But in this case I started the play. My first call went to the Secret Service's Tactical Center. I saved Jimmy Carter's Georgia bacon once, and I've worked with 'em a few times since. They listen to me, pronto. I imagine the state Adjutant General got told to listen to Curt, no questions asked."

He must have been right. Not five minutes later a large convoy roared up behind us. A single HumVee pulled even with us. Of all things a white flag flew out the passenger window.

The Voice used the speaker function of the rig's CB radio to give a few instructions. The white flag disappeared. The HumVee's four way hazard flashers went on as the driver floored the gas. The convoy soon passed out of sight ahead of us.

Fifteen minutes later we pulled onto a county road through a National Guard roadblock. We headed west. A couple inbound of Guard deuce-and-a-half trucks pulled off the road to give us a wide berth. Civilians filled the covered cargo areas. Other Guard vehicles jumped aside as we approached.

"Its like that Richard Pryor quote," the Voice laughed. "When you're on fire, people *will* get out of your way."

I didn't say anything. All my attention centered on the growing fireballs within the trailer. Then I saw the large hill containing the quarry. The thing rose about three hundred feet above the surrounding area. Beginning generations ago men removed one side of the hill in a pie-shaped hundred and twenty degree wedge. Then they began to blast below ground level.

The Voice headed the big rig down the ramp to the bottom. He barely managed a left turn as the ramp ended. He somehow jockeyed the rig down another forty feet without tipping over. Finally he parked with the ball bearing side of the trailer angled to one "straight" side of the pie shape cut. When the charge cut loose the shrapnel would bounce off that wall, and into the other wall before having a chance to head out of the quarry. We hoped.

The expansion of the fertilizer blast continued. I walked back and forth and around the truck. I felt like my blood was on fire. I knew if I sat down I'd pass out. When that happened... BOOM!

The Voice called Van Loan again. What could get us out of the mess I didn't know. I could now feel heat radiating from the body of the trailer. The metal sides soon became far too hot to touch. Gas and vapor began to hiss, then whistle through every crack, crevice and pinhole in the big rig. From things some of the fire guys once told me at Silo's, I figured the worst thing I could do would be open the doors. I couldn't possibly control a backdraft.

The Voice activated the speaker feature of the Iridium phone. I heard Curt Van Loan's voice, "I've got help on the way. Can he hold out for half an hour?"

The Voice turned his veiled face towards me. "I hope so," was all I could say.

Pretend you are walking on broken glass barefooted. Pretend your skin's being scrubbed with a wire brush. Pretend your head is spinning. Pretend you hold a porcupine in your bare hands as you try to squeeze him hard enough to keep his spines from coming out. Now imagine that all those things get more intense and more painful by the minute. I started counting the laps as I walked around the truck. After about twenty I lost count.

The Voice hovered around me for a time. At first it felt good. Then it began to bother me. Finally I waved him away. I didn't dare speak. A moment after that I felt the load in the trailer begin to shift. I tried to squeeze that porcupine to the size of a ping-pong ball. I felt like a hundred Tasers hit my body. I reeled. Out of nowhere the Voice's hands stabilized my spinning body. I held on. He never realized just how close he came to being vaporized. The load steadied. That's when I realized that some of the barrels must have melted. Liquid Hell now sloshed around inside the trailer as the temperature kept rising. Some of that liquid began to drip, pour, and even spray from different parts of the truck.

The satellite phone came to life again. I jumped, but not much. I wondered in passing just what expression the Voice actually wore.

"Ask him how far away he can maintain control."

I didn't trust myself to speak. I signed, "No more than five hundred yards."

The Voice relayed that.

Van Loan replied, "Hang on. They're less that five minutes out. Can you be sure you won't jam a turbo-jet?"

"Not if its already going," I signed. "Five I can make. But probably not seven."

After translation Van Loan replied, "Understood. Good luck!"

Those last few minutes the Voice walked behind me. With one hand he held my belt. The other kept a grip on my collar. He held me upright as I swayed from side to side. Just when I felt ready to fall over backwards we heard it.

A long black helicopter roared over the lip of the ridge faster than seemed possible to my addled mind. The Voice half carried me up the inclined side of the pit to a flat area. I could feel my grip starting to loosen just a tiny bit as the chopper bounced to a landing. A heavyset figure in black coveralls and a weird looking flight helmet jumped out. He rushed over.

"Get him aboard, but gently," the Voice told the newcomer.

Each one grabbed an arm. I felt like I was floating. Quickly I was strapped to a pull down canvas seat in the very cramped interior of the helicopter. The Voice simply put his back to a bulkhead as the air crewman flipped switches on an instrument board. I felt the chopper lift off. Very slowly it drifted away from the highest point of the ridge around the bowl's pie-shaped quarry. I squeezed the blessed porcupine to the size of an M&M. I raised my cupped hands.

"Hold," came the aircrew's voice. The chopper paused. I felt it turn back toward the truck.

"Is that it?" asked the Voice. I nodded.

I heard the heavyset guy say, "Let's go. Nap of the Earth."

The chopper began to accelerate. A lot. I felt us pass almost directly over the truck as the craft gained speed. Then it dived just a bit. I felt the ridge of the hill come between me and the truck. I somehow managed to squeeze just a little bit harder.

Then, just inside my limit of control, the aircrew called, "Punch it, String!"

Acceleration twice that of Van Loan's jet slammed me back. I felt my control beginning to slip a second or two before I blacked out.


I swam out of the darkness. About half conscious I mentally grabbed for the explosives. I learned two things. I could feel no explosives in the area. Plus my left arm was tied down. I opened my eyes. I looked out through the goggles of my uniform. I lay with my upper body propped up in a large tent. An I-V tube ran into my arm. Not again, I thought.

I looked around. Three chairs at a table to my left held people in camouflage uniforms. One pointed at me. All rose. A woman wearing a Major's oak leaves and a full Colonel approached me. The woman had a caduceus on her collar and the name "Fryan" on her uniform. She gave me a quick check, then withdrew a few steps.

The Colonel said, "How are you feeling?" Then he squeezed the area around his Adam's apple. In barely a whisper the incredible croaking of the Voice assured me, "Everything's under control." Then he squeezed the same spot again.

"I feel a bit numb," I replied. "How long was I out?"

"Almost eight hours," said the doctor. "As exhausted as you were I expected you to be out at least another twelve."

Still hovering over me, the Voice finger spelled a shielded "OK to talk. But no ID."

"Believe it or not, doctor, that's by far the longest I've slept in years."

"Now that is strange," said Dr. Fryan. "You are still a bit dehydrated. And your electrolytes were almost non-existent. You need at least one more bag of fluid."

The third person left the table to squat down beside me. Two stars adorned his collar.

"I'm the state's Adjutant General. Thanks to your help the Guard could evacuate everyone in the area of the explosion. I'm told I can't ask any questions, but I sure can offer my thanks." With that he extended his hand.

Not too long after that the Voice and I were alone in the tent.

"How's it feel to be part of a non-existent military unit? We'll get you out as soon as you can travel. Is there anything you want to know?"

"The explosion? How big?" was all I managed.

"Only about forty per cent of what it should have been. All that heat and vented gas must have done it. I'll bet you wouldn't want to try that again."

"Maybe I couldn't, if I wanted to," I replied. "I may have burned myself out. You're probably packing. The general had a sidearm. And there's a rack of M-16's over there. Unless nobody has ammo, I can't feel any of them. And I can't sync with the generator outside, at all."

"Maybe you just need more rest," said the Voice. "Then again, if you never change another chemical reaction in your life, you saved maybe seventy thousand lives. I'd say that would be a fair trade-off."

And I agreed with him.

August 1974, Richard Nixon resigned the Presidency of the United States of America. The first of a new generation of Independent Operators became active to deal with possible fall-out from that unprecedented situation. A few years later this same Independent Operator broke up an assassination plot against James Earl Carter. The public never hears of this, but the Secret Service, and others, take note.

Soon after this Independent Operator comes into my life. Back into my life, actually. For this deadly Agent of Justice saved my life not only here in my home town, but in Saigon, as well. What does he look like? Nobody knows. Anybody who has knowingly met him calls him the Voice. For his extremely rare public speech sounds like nothing else in the annals of history.

I don't know much more than that. And I am what passes for his biographer. Plus, maybe a bit of a therapist, too. Most of his work involves gathering information on people who make life worse. Criminals, bad or incompetent politicians, and public servants, societal bullies, it doesn't matter. He finds the dirt and turns it over to the police, prosecutors, or the media.

My name is Erwin K. Roberts. I worked in Saigon for Havens International Media. Stateside I became editor of the local paper in the Clarion newspaper chain. When the Voice popped up in my life in recent decades it was usually to relate a story. A case that hasn't gone as expected. Or got too big. For when lives are on the line he becomes about the most deadly man in the world. Yet, he truly hates to kill. Letting me write up his exploits seems to help him get it off his chest.

The Voice stayed active from 1974 until at least December of 1999. I last heard from him after a very tragic case. He may have moved his operations elsewhere. He may have retired. If he did retire, the woman he let into his life in this 1989 case probably helped make it happen.

# Crime Of The Arts

PART 1

## Probing the City

September 21, 1989

Well, here I sit. Nobody's taken a shot at me for the last fifteen minutes. Half way up the side of one of the rockier Rocky Mountains. Being looked for by a squad of Rambo wantta-be's.

I'm surprised the girl hasn't started to panic. This was going to be such a simple operation. Just roust some rich twenty-something who gives drugs to girls so he and his friends can party. Now I wish I had more ammo, warmer clothing. Euell Gibbons should drop by and tell me just *which* parts of these pine trees are edible. How do I get myself into these things?

September 16, 1989

It all started when two mid-level drug wholesalers sat down for their regular lunch. One worked the northern suburbs. The other's territory covered the southern side. These guys had a few more practical brain cells than most. With all the territories between them they had little chance of conflict. They realized that they shared common problems. I'm not saying they were totally honest with each other, but both benefited by sharing information and gossip about the local trade. I had both of them pretty well wired. I mean if somebody's got to deal drugs, I rather have them than lots of others. Neither wanted the problems that territorial expansion would cause. Both simply supplied a demand and did nothing much to increase that demand. That's why I only had them on my watch list.

The information I picked up from them often gave me the angle I needed to attack other, less restrained operators. When they become the most dangerous drug wholesalers in town by default, then I'll go after them. Anyway, I almost always attended their luncheons, one way, or another.

That day it was easy. They had lunch at a private booth at the back of a Thai restaurant. The owner mixed Thai decorations with American Bizarre. My bug sat between them on the booth wall, hardwired into the nose of a Jackalope.

The talk meandered as usual. About this cop, about that supplier, who's in jail, who's out, what drug's going up, which is declining in use. Then it got interesting.

"I hear one of Jake's boys in midtown ran into problems selling to people at the Girls' Shelter," remarked Mr. North-side. "They say he saw a couple of his regular customers there. Started to talk to them and got run off by a couple of big toughs in crew-cuts. I mean who wears crew-cuts but Marines."

"Hadn't heard that part," said South-side, cutting at his Thai spiced Prime Rib. "Fits though. Seems th' Parker runs that place buys from one of my people. Down in my territory. Parker called my guy. Said he's happy with the quality and price and could we arrange that the shelter was off limits to every local street guy. I called Jake. Jake now gets a grand, direct, a month to keep that block clear. Really no big deal. Most of th' broads are trying to get clean anyways, while they're there. Most don't stay clean in the long run, so... "

Well, I kept on recording, but I stopped listening. Mentally I called up a metro map and tried to remember what Jake's territory currently consisted of. Unlike those two, Jake always has a minor turf war or two going on. Jake likes to recruit new users. Jake's on my prime list of people we can do without.

When the luncheon broke up I found a safe phone and dialed a non-existent phone number. In the back room of Sanchez Electronics & Communications an answering machine picked up and immediately beeped. "Midtown. Drug wholesaler: Jake. Addresses all fitting Girl's Shelter his territory."

George Sanchez's business keeps him pretty busy these days, but he always comes through. Knowing I'd have an answer pretty soon, I hurried to do the other things I'd planed for the day.

That evening I prepared a Snare Package in one of my apartments. The DA would love the night scope enhanced shots of a package exchange between two supposed enemies. I'd left the short-wave radio system up and running rather than recording. George's encoded signal came through the decoder, ran to the text processor of the Commodore 64 computer, then out to the noisy printer. I made a mental note to upgrade to a better system with a quieter printer.

The list was short. Since neither the Catholic, nor the Buddhist operations were likely to have crew-cut bouncers I checked them off. That left two. A couple of phone calls later I figured that the Renaissance Shelter for Troubled Women sat in my bulls-eye.

September 17, 1989

The following morning I wrapped up a few loose ends of other matters, then went down to Silly… er… City Hall.

Professor Simon Archer is emeritus at the local University. He writes articles and whole books on city planning. Outside his field he is woefully absentminded. Whenever I need to research something at the Hall, Professor Archer visits. I flitted from office to office collecting data.

Back at the apartment I went over plats, blue prints, deeds, street and utility plans. The Anson Foundation for the Fine Arts owned the whole block that contained the Renaissance Shelter for Troubled Women. The Anson family I knew. Old money, local roots to the beginning of the city. Did lots of good works, many without publicity. Their Foundation for the Fine Arts? New, to me.

The shelter consisted of several connected storefronts and the living space above them. The Foundation seemed to be renting some of the other storefronts. One of the rented buildings had been a notorious Speakeasy during Prohibition. Red flag that. Speakeasies often came with extracurricular architectural features. Some of the buildings across the alley were marked empty, or as storage for the Foundation. Time to take a look.

I buzzed across town in my special van. Years ago, George Sanchez dubbed it the Imagemaker because of the makeup gear and clothing racks it carries. At my hidden garage I changed faces and put on a Gas Company uniform. Nobody but the guilty and the crazy turn down a natural gas inspection. I rigged up a work truck with the right decals and antennae and motored over to the shelter.

I'd selected the Gas Company employee's personality carefully. A nice guy, neither handsome, nor ugly. I gave him just a bit of the aw-shucks. He hadn't fallen off the Turnip Truck today, but it hadn't been long either. I parked the truck, grabbed the stack of test gear that looked just like what the Gas Company really used, and entered.

I almost thought I'd entered a hotel lobby. A few of the nice chairs and couches contained young women. None appeared over thirty. Mostly they seemed to be studying.

A black woman of about twenty-five stood behind the reception counter. She seemed weary at first. She relaxed as I managed to "ma'am" her about four times while asking to see the manager. She used an honest to Lily Tomlin, Stromberg-Carlson plug operated switchboard to summon her manager.

"I'm Mrs. O'Toole. Can I help you?"

"Yes, ma'am, I'm Joseph Byers," I began with a big smile. "Somebody called in and said they smelled gas while walking by here. So they sent me over. Did anyone tell you all?"

"No, Mr. Byers," she got all formal. "This person called you, but didn't step in to warn us. Seems strange."

"Sure does, ma'am. Probably someone pulling a prank. But I gotta treat every call like its real. Hate to turn on the Ten O'clock News and find out this place went inta' orbit. Now the Company'd prefer you get everyone out of the building, but I can't tell you to until I find a leak. 's up to you ma'am."

"I think we will stay until you do," she said a little coolly. She stepped to the switchboard connected a cable and pushed the ringer switch forward three quick times. A few seconds later I met the crew-cuts.

One turned out to be Matthew, the other James. Big, bulked up, and not a hint of a smile to be seen. I began to wonder if I'd find big pods in the basement. O'Toole assigned James to take me around, while Matthew would tell all occupants of the potential problem.

I had James take me out in the alley to look at the meters. I waved my detectors around. They looked just like the Gas Company's because they had the same cases. George Sanchez took out the perfectly good guts of the things and replaced them with much smaller (and much higher $$$) electronics. Then he started adding the fun stuff. Echo-locators, transmitters, metal detectors. I waved them all over the alley. If there had been a gas leak, I'd have found that too. Noting the small number of gas meters, I asked James about that.

"When they rebuilt for the shelter," he told me, "they ran four buildings into one. I'll show you the only furnace next."

We went back inside. As we started down to the basement, James paused and pushed an intercom button. "Ladies, me and the Gas man coming down." He turned to me, "We'll give 'em a minute. They sometimes fit clothes and try them on." Good way to hide something, too, I decided.

We exited the stairwell into a multipurpose room. Obviously both classroom and recreation center with blackboard, study chairs, and some old video and non-electronic games. Several girls seemed to be studying while others took a break around a table. The window dressing ran much like upstairs, but subtle differences came at me from all directions. James hurried me to the utility room while I apologized to all the ma'ams for interrupting. Upstairs the studiousness seemed real. Down here... a sham.

James got a little uneasy as I inspected the furnace and pipes closely. I threw every logical question I could think of about the condition of these buildings at him. I didn't try scare tactics on him. For all I knew he might understand more about the behavior of natural gas than I did.

He glowered around at the girls as we went back up stairs. None of them seemed to have moved or even eaten any of the snacks at the one table. I ma'amed them again and turned to smile at each group. One of these days George is going to manage to get a TV camera crammed into the hard hat I wore. 'Til then I'll continue to rely on my memory sessions. Though he obviously preferred not to, James agreed to a quick swing around the upper floors.

I thanked everyone and departed. As soon as I knew I had no tail I stopped at a phone booth and called George. I told him to hack my visit into the Gas Company's computer call record in case someone checked up on me. Then I hightailed it to one of my quiet places.

Seated in what amounted to a walk-in closet, I dimmed the lights. On the table in front of me sat a small art deco decorative lamp. The outside is a cylinder of glass with a pattern painted on it. Inside is another translucent cylinder with a contrasting pattern. The heat from the bulb soon set the inner one turning throwing dim moire patterns around the room. I used this as my focus.

The technique is supposed to have come from Tibet, but one of my honorary Uncles taught it to me as a kid. Soon I disconnected from the here and now and scanned my memory back to the shelter and to the girls in the basement. I studied each face closely, even putting myself on pause, or in a loop. Most people might notice some nervousness in those women. Having been around the underbelly (love that word) of society for so long, I saw more. Everyone of them I had gotten a good look at seemed to be on something. There were ticks, eye pupils dilated wrong, sweats, other things. And not all on the same thing.

With that conclusion I "ran" my memory upstairs and compared them to the bunch on public display. If anyone upstairs had taken so much as an aspirin, I couldn't detect it.

As my memory ran forward again, I picked up a pen and started making notes and sketches of where I'd probed with my instruments.

Two hours, and two cans of Mountain Dew later, I let myself into the basement of George's business. I signaled my presence and began hooking up the Gas detectors for download. I'm not half bad at reading this stuff, but George is much better.

George joined me a bit later. He does move fast these days. His wheelchair is long gone and I sometimes swear he uses that cane for a pogo-stick. We used to meet in a forgotten bomb shelter at his home. For all I'd helped the family out, I knew I scared his mother half to death. Now he's on his own, making a public name for himself in electronic security. And he's still my ace in the hole.

He looked over my sketches while the data downloaded and processed. Finally the PaintJet printer started printing a series of images and text. While we waited George told me that he'd gone through some newsgroup archives and BBS's about Women's shelters. The Renaissance Shelter for Troubled Women had a reputation for going its own way. They seemed to believe in starting people over in places far away from their troubles. They got their clients jobs two, three, even four states over. That was not to say that they were trying to only run troubled people out of town. They accepted transfers from other shelters and served as the last step to independence for them. Mrs. O'Toole had a reputation for making some odd choices in who to take in.

Finally we attacked the readouts, along with the Professor's plats and plans. Lots of interesting tidbits showed up, but the big one, as I'd suspected, was some kind of tunnel under the alley. Of course the thing could be walled off at both ends and be emptier than Capone's Vault. (Poor Geraldo, he never knew I got there first.)

All this meant I had to get into those empty and storage places on the backside of the alley. I ought to get a room in that seedy five-story hotel a block over and study the place. For some reason I didn't want to wait that long. I never leave weapons or other question producing stuff at George's. So I told him good-by and headed to the place closest to the shelter where I keep a full set of assault gear. I'd catch a nap until everyone in that block *should* be asleep.

September 18, 1989, 12:47 A.M.

The whole upper floor was dark as I let myself down a slim rope from the skylight. Empty of people, too, as my night-vision goggles showed. I'd detected no alarms electronically. Seen no infrared beams with special filters. Nothing flashed, rang, or exploded when I quietly touched the floor. This loft seemed to cover about two-thirds of the building's top floor. Though the loft was empty, I could feel life somewhere else. I set out to explore.

An artist's loft. Well, several artists. There were setups for painting, sculpture, even a welded something that looked like Salvador Dali had set off an explosion in a porcupine. There was no way into the other part of the floor. I decided to use one exposure from my infrared light equipped camera on the metal thing. I might never see the like of it again if I lived to be one hundred.

As I crept down the stairs I took stock again. I had a young nondescript face. Under my infiltration coveralls and vail I wore a suit with a reversible coat, reversible collar, and such that it had several possible looks. In one pocket of my pack I carried a quick attach mask that fit a beefy face over my current one, plus a zipper-suit that looked like a city Police Department uniform, if you didn't get too close.

For weapons I had my gas gun, two throwing knives, a few gas and smoke bombs, plus a Smith & Wesson 9 millimeter with several magazines. The camera looked like a fancy sort of tape player. The special plastic let the IR light through like glass.

The stairwell looped back at the second floor level, but didn't have an entrance. I continued down. I hugged the walls as I got lower. At the end of the stairs was a door with a small window and panic hardware attached. After listening to silence for a minute or two, I peeked out the window into a vestibule. To the right stood a door into the first floor. In front was the formidable looking street door I'd seen form the other side. A heavy metal bar with thick brackets hung across it. Glad I didn't try to pick that.

The door to the loft held a simple alarm that I bypassed. I seemed to be on the protected side. I cracked the stair door and looked for cameras. None. Quickly I looked at the door to the main area. Needed some work, but doable. Two alarms that George's gadgets could handle. I turned off the vestibule light and got to work.

Soon I crouched in a darkened, glassed in, office looking out at a large mood lit open area. The office must have been for a commercial U-Store-It before the new owners. Heavy wire cages started at the office and went around the perimeter. Some of the cages were still full of boxes and whatnot. I could see where cages had been on the main floor, but they were gone. In their place were a few high quality tables and chairs sitting on expensive looking Asian carpets.

Seated at a couple of the tables were well dressed men with smug and contented looks. Behind a well stocked bar stood Matthew. He looked bored. Opposite the office a door opened, held by James. A man of forty-some came out with a girl on his arm. She wore a domino mask and a filmy veil and about as much more as a Vegas showgirl. I pressed the camera against the glass and tripped the shutter. The man led the exotically dressed woman to one of the cages I had a bad angle on. He made a great show of ushering her in. Then he stepped to the bar where Matthew held out a glass on a tray.

I saw Matthew glance at his watch. I barely heard as he called out, "Last call, gentlemen! The bus leaves in ten minutes. James, please get them started upstairs."

James departed and soon couples began emerging from that other door. The girls all ended up in that one cage I couldn't see into. When James reappeared he made a signal. It must have been the all clear because Matthew started giving orders while I changed film packs.

"Gentlemen, please, you all know the drill. Line up by the bar and put your hoods on. Anyone can't make it speak up. James will carry you. Fireman's carry, you'll be happier walking… OK, arms on the shoulder in front of you. James lead the way.

James started off at a nice shuffle pace. The hooded revelers followed. They went round and round, here and there. Even cold sober they'd be lost. That conga line seemed worth the first frame of fresh film.

Matthew, meanwhile, walked over to a spot on the far wall and moved a large bulletin board aside. He opened a door I hadn't noticed and stepped into the dark. A moment later he flicked on a light. I saw a vehicle about the size and shape of a medium UPS truck with the door rolled up. Quickly I used the "tape player's" volume dial to change to the telescopic lens. I pointed and prayed.

A little set of stairs with duel handrails allowed James to finally lead the men into the truck without trouble. As the door rolled down I noticed a medium sized recreational vehicle further on. The door between the buildings closed.

I crept out of the office. Very faintly I could hear the truck's engine start. I got my gas gun out and flipped up the mixing head. This gave me longer range, but less volume. The two liquids that create Dad's binary gas would mix on impact, water gun style. Using a pillar for cover, I hoped both Matthew and James went with the truck.

I peered around the pillar into the cage the women had gone into.

Empty! Well, now I knew where one exit of the bootlegger's tunnel was.

Still with an eye and ear out for one of the crew-cuts, I gave the place a quick once over. Some marks hinted that the bar rolled into one of the cages. I'd have bet the rest of the trappings did too.

Up to the second floor. No visible way to the third floor. No cages, but storerooms with fancy double key locks. I didn't pick any. I had an idea what I'd find.

I slipped back downstairs. Still no one home. I decided to find the other part of the loft.

It took me five ear-straining minutes to discover the door and two more to find the release that swung the in-wall heating unit outward. I crept up the concealed stairs.

Sometimes I get so lucky I scare myself. The first room was an office. A light flashed by the phone on the desk. The marker read "Open Door." The second room was a tiny apartment. A light flashed next to that phone also. My heart pounded for a moment. I re-gripped the gas-gun and slid out one of my throwing knives. As I eased the next door open I heard a distant soft thud, and a whimper. Another artist's studio. Only a couple of lights at the far end were on. I could hear harsh breathing now.

My eyes adjusted a bit. I noticed a tiny amount of pulsing light. A wadded woman's skirt covered it.

Just as I stepped forward, I heard a strangled roar, "Why did you do it? You were perfect for me. Why did you change you…" Trying not to trip over anything, I moved forward. The outraged man questioned his companion's pure human genetics, ancestry, and personal habits. Then he roared "I'll just have to use you without…"

I'd moved around a screen, the last thing blocking my view. A man stood over a woman chained in a chair. Blood covered or spattered what little I could see of her. I triggered the gas-gun just as he raised a big piece of two-by-four.

My mind sort of detached itself from normal speed. The gas would never take him down before he crushed the woman's skull. I was too far away to tackle him in time. Can't possibly draw the 9MM fast enough. The knife! Got'ta throw the knife.

That's when I realized my hand was empty. Glancing forward I saw the knife finish its revolution before sliding between two of the man's upper ribs.

Like a near death experience I watched my body move forward to yank the man away from the girl. She looked up at my veiled face then slumped unconscious.

Only then did I realize I still held the trigger of the gas-gun in a death grip. Enough gas swirled around the room to take down two elephants, three hippos, and one rhino, with enough left over for James and Matthew.

Body and mind now came back together. The glimpse of the girl. I shuddered. Better check the man. If he wasn't dead, he'd soon be unconscious. No he was dead. Beautiful throw, even if I don't remember making it.

Then I forced myself to look at the girl. From what I could see, there was not a mark on her body. The chains were even padded. No pinch or chafe marks. But the face…

The last time I saw a face that shredded involved a Bouncing Betty Land Mine in Viet Nam, and instant death. But she was alive. A miracle that both of her eyes seemed to be intact. I covered her with bedding I grabbed from the apartment to prevent shock.

Before I used the phone I stopped and looked closely at the man. Well, I had met the Parker. Parker. Short for Poplar Park. Where old money lives in this town. William George Edward Anson, the Third, of the young Parker Generation. Executive Director of the Renaissance Shelter for Troubled Women. Pimp, drug purveyor, sure, but what else?

When James and Matthew get back I'm going to find some answers.

Part 2:
# Damsel Rescued, Now What?

September 21, 1989

Dana caught a few minutes rest while I did a little scrounging. At least three survivalists still pursued us. Even if I found the right materials I didn't have time to put together any of the fancy traps I learned about in Viet Nam. Some of Dad's Indian friends used to take me with them on survival hikes. They didn't see much good in snares and traps. They preferred not to leave a trail to be followed.

Dana, between her rage and the drugs in her system, doggedly continued, presuming she could go on indefinitely. Rage can motivate the mind for a long time, but her body simply could not handle much more. For the hundredth time I cursed the bright idea that caused me to bring her along. Seemed like a good idea at the time. A little rough and ready financial justice that backfired. How do I get myself into these messes?

I'd overheard how a super-yuppie seemed to be supplying drugs to the residents of a women's shelter. My recon of the place showed the shelter housed two classes of clients, the medicated and the un-medicated. Backed up to the shelter and controlled by the same old money family sat a storage building. The evening I slipped in there I discovered that aside from some artists' loft studio space, the two crew-cut bouncers... er... security guards from they women's shelter operated a covert bordello using the drugged women they theoretically protected.

In a hidden part of the loft I located William George Edward Anson, the Third, the rich young lunatic who ran the show. Just in time to stop him from killing Dana with a two by four. With the mastermind dead, I started trying to put the pieces together.

September 18, 1989 Very Early Morning

I took stock quickly. James and Matthew, the bouncers, could return any time. The girl needed medical attention. She wasn't bleeding. At least not now. The gas cloud I'd overenthusiasticly let loose in the studio would keep her out for at least two hours, maybe more. She'd better wake up in friendly medical hands. I had no idea what her mental state would be or what drugs still polluted her body. I hoped for the best. That look she gave me before she passed out had not been fear, but relief. Not surprise, either. What she'd seen amounted to a ninja with a smoking Buck Rogers style ray gun assaulting the man who'd turned her face to hamburger. Relief, maybe, but no surprise seemed unusual.

The chair the girl was chained to had wheels. I pushed it back through the apartment and into the office where I could watch both her and the stairs to the second floor. Medical help meant two possibilities. I started both.

I grabbed the phone and punched up one of my throwaway phone numbers. George Sanchez could make a fortune with the gadgets he builds for me. That phone can be programmed remotely to make calls that are hard to trace. If they are, the phone self destructs better than the old 'Mission:Impossible' tape recorders. I entered the map coordinates of a spot two blocks over, then two command codes.

Doc Wannamaker's on call ambulance would head to the designated spot immediately, from way out in the suburbs. The other command, request really, went to the pager of a paramedic universally known as 'Tiny.' About the size of the Incredible Hulk, Tiny knows more about the Voice than anyone outside my inner circle. A conscientious objector who served two tours of Viet Nam as a medic, he wouldn't hurt a fly. Except to protect a patient. He understands what I do. If possible, Tiny comes.

I slipped down the stairs and closed the concealed door. On the desk the flashing warning light went out. I followed the wires from the light to an old wood humidor. Opening it revealed a security control panel. 'The Third' could monitor the whole building

For some reason I didn't want to have this go public. Not yet. Too many mysteries unsolved. Too many mysteries would stay unsolved. The Anson family hates publicity. They would work hard to bury a detailed investigation. However many women had been exploited by this operation would need to be found and helped. I suspected the shelter did do some good. I wanted that to continue, and be expanded. The Anson's could well afford that.

I checked the girl's vital signs again. Then I moved the chair under a light where I could watch the security panel. She'd been drugged or unconscious when put in the chair. Had to be. No signs of struggle and 'The Third' went to great trouble not to mark her body. Her arms, legs, and waist padded before the chains were locked on. Then the chains were taped to the pads. Her neck remained upright, held by some of that hard to find four inch wide adhesive tape.

Then she'd had to sit there and take the beatings. Some of the marks had to be two or three days old.

A place like this had to have a set of bolt cutters, but I might not find them for a week. I grabbed the set of picks from my kit and got to work. The first lock took a bit. The second fell open as I started to probe. And the third. Five locks keyed alike. With a chill running down my spine I realized that this had all happened before.

I carried the girl to the couch. Checked vitals and wrapped her warmly. Mentally I took a couple of turns of restraint around my temper. I needed the crew cuts alive and not heavily damaged. Right now I felt like filleting them with a nail file.

Something vibrated behind my right kidney. Tiny's "I'm in position" page. Thank God he'd been close.

I took one more look at the girl. I couldn't tell if she'd been pretty or not. It would be a long time before she came close to looking normal. Wannamaker would help. He makes lots of money from people who can afford it. They dry out, or otherwise get their heads screwed on straight, at his "Spa" with no publicity. Using that cash to help the down and out gives his life joy. The girl, (Blast! What *is* her name?) represented a long term project. Doc loves a challenge.

I'd be taking a chance carrying her on the street. Then inspiration struck. I'd noticed several full sized pose-able artist's mannequins in the studio. I sprinted to the nearest one and yanked an arm off. Then I tied her corresponding arm to her side. I slipped off my sniper's veil and turned it inside out. In the dark, the lighter side of the fabric would look somewhat like the color of the loose arm. I carefully fitted the mask over her face. Now I hoped I looked like I lugged a busted mannequin.

I carried her downstairs and put her on one of the party tables. Quickly I rigged the biggest gas bomb I carried to the door from the hidden garage to the 'storage facility.' If the crew cuts came back, I'd find them stretched out on the floor waiting.

Carrying her got more awkward. I held the false arm in one hand and my 9 millimeter in the other. I'd opened the front of the coveralls. The face was a throwaway that did not matter.

I rotated the huge steel bar of the pedestrian door and stepped out on the sidewalk. To silence. Three blocks north a car headed away from us. I moved south and across the street. My stride said I was in no hurry and had every right to be there. I hoped I played to an empty stage.

I spotted the nose of Tiny's van sticking out of an alley in the target block. I increased my pace. Not only did I want the girl in good hands, but I wanted to greet Matthew and James personally.

I approached the van softly whistling a certain tune. Seeing no one I spoke the monthly signal in Vietnamese. Tiny materialized out of a shadow. For a guy that makes Arnold look puny, Tiny can blend in like few others.

He silently opened the rear of the van and took the girl from me. One huge step and he put her gently down on the bed. The interior of the van looks like a cross between a conversion job and a throwback to the VW cracker-box hippie vans of the sixties. Hidden away, the gear of a mini-emergency room can handle the initial treatment of most trauma. I know. More than once I've felt those powerful arms settle me into that same bed.

To Tiny's unspoken question I began by telling about the drugs I suspected she'd been given. As I spoke I removed the veil and showed him her face.

Like a lot of Viet Nam era GI's, Tiny can curse in several languages. As he quickly triaged her I recognized Vietnamese, Chinese, Montanyard, Pigeon, Tagalog, and tried to identify a couple of others. As I waved good-by he had the scrambled radio phone shoulder held to his ear while he unpacked an IV kit and other things he figured Doc Wannamaker would ask for. As soon as possible he'd transfer to Doc's ambulance. Doc's fully qualified EMT's also pack heat. Lots of heat. Tiny wouldn't leave her until he'd consulted with Doc personally.

I stood on a corner where I could see both Tiny's van and the garage entrance. The wait seemed forever, but can't have been long. Finally Tiny pulled out, legal and safely, but definitely making tracks. I knew he'd set a new meeting point with Doc's crew.

I had to restrain myself from sprinting back to the storage building. Dog-legging to the Imagemaker, I grabbed a couple of kits from the racks. Kits too big to carry in a tactical assault, but now I controlled the beachhead. I didn't know where the crew-cuts had driven their load of semi-inebriated customers, but it had to be at least to Poplar Park.

Only one way to keep this mess quiet I'd decided. Got to bring The Third back to life.

If the crew-cuts came in some other way than how they'd left I felt pretty sure the security board would tell me. My next project wouldn't wait. I hurried up to the hidden loft. Anson hadn't bleed much. I dragged him into the office and got to work. The face kit lets me fashion masks of real people. Usually the subject is asleep, not dead. Dead is easier some ways and harder in others. Several quick photos, including stereoscopes. No facial hair other than the eyebrows. Good. I found a razor and gave him a quick shave. Then layers of chemicals. Release compound. Rubber-like mold, first painted on, then poured into a frame fitted around the head. No straw holes to breathe through this time.

Let the face set. Start on the hands with some of the same stuff. Did the crew cuts stop for a beer?

Chemically enforced break-time. I fiddle with my throat implant to get as close to the Parker's voice as possible. Hope I can find recordings to work with. Don't want to fall back on the old "I just swallowed something crooked" routine.

"Watson, you see, but you do not observe," remarked the First Master Detective. Especially when I'm in a hurry. I'd wandered back into the studio. There sat not one, but two video cameras on tripods. No tapes in them.

Back in the office I found drawers full. Most were carefully labeled. Titles like "Collins-Painter" and "Boise-Metal Sculpture." I popped one in the VCR. Basically Anson interviewed the artists working in the other loft on the creative process. Why do this instead of that. Just what I needed for voice checks.

Before I started working on the voice matching I noticed a couple of unmarked tapes sitting next to a commercial tape eraser across the room. The hidden loft appeared on the screen this time. Anson directed a girl as she reclined on a couch. Named Marty, she giggled a lot. Apparently unused to the attention she reveled in Anson's interest. She carried a few too many pounds by today's standards, but Anson claimed to like that. He seemed to be trying to match her position to something off camera. The pose looked vaguely familiar.

The second tape brought me to a halt. This had to be the girl. She seemed slightly out of it, but had a droll sense of humor. Anson posed her on a short pedestal. Seated with her legs folded he had her working her arms like a Thai dancer. Her face had been neither beautiful nor ugly. Sort of a nice average. What I had not suspected was the definite Asian look of her eyes. I learned her name: Dana.

At one point Anson told her, "With your eyes fixed you look just like her." To which Dana replied, "I still don't like them much. I thought I did them for Mr. Youshida, not you."

Anson took a deep breath at that. Controlling his temper I

decided. Very useful information for my role playing. Finally he continued, "I suggested it to Youshida San. He thought it wonderfully ironic. Several girls in his Kyoto office had their eyes Westernized. Part of a fad. To have his Western mistress go Asian delighted him. Besides, what does it matter? It gets you all those pills you love. But I promise, when you've finished modeling for my sculpture I'll take you to get them changed back. If you still want to."

Considering Anson's final words: "I'll just have to use you without..." That last statement gave me shivers.

I'd let the content of the tape take too much of my attention. As I turned my head I noticed a light flashing on the security monitor. I looked at the legend: Garage Door. How long had that been on?

I hit the stop button on the remote. I tossed it on to the desk as I passed. Quietly as I could I bolted down the stairs. Before I started on the last flight I held the nine millimeter automatic in one hand and a throwing knife in the other. I need not have bothered. Five steps from street level I heard the distinctive pop of the big gas bomb.

With an evil word or two on my lips I sat down on a stair tread until the coughing stopped. My father's old binary knockout gas has this great bonus feature. The first whiff into the nostrils causes most people to take a deep breath. James and Matthew were no exceptions. I found them snoring on the floor. I'd wanted them scared and sweating, confronted by an outraged relative of one of the girls. Oh, well! Change of plans number two hundred and thirty four in a series. Collect them all.

I pulled out the gas gun. I blew a make-sure dose up their noses. Then I walked through the open door into the very well equipped garage. Apparently the crew cuts did all the work on the truck and the RV. That meant secrets.

The RV stretched about 30 feet. In the glove box I found the registration, and a wallet full of Anson's pictures with another name attached. Below that were a number of speeding tickets and some letters from a lawyer in Gunsight, Colorado, to a post box in Colorado Springs. The solicitor stated that tickets thus and so were taken care of. All the ticket locations followed the shortest run from here to the Gunsight area.

The interior of the RV seemed ordinary. Too ordinary for your up-scale Poplar Parker like Anson. And there was something else. Finally I decided that the ceiling seemed lower than other RVs I'd been in.

Then I realized that the vehicle vibrated more than it should. There was no noise, but the vibes came through my feet. Quickly I centered my search on the queen sized bed. I tossed the mattress and bedding aside. It took five minutes to figure how unlatch the hard surface underneath. Finally half the area lifted up with a big hiss. Cold air rushed over me. The open space turned out to be coffin sized and accounted for the raised floor. A small thermometer read 34 degrees. Empty. I closed it. A few seconds later the other side opened at my touch. Inside I found Marty.

I hate to say it, but she looked peaceful. Like she had gone to sleep happy. She was in a robe that seemed to be from the nineteenth century. I said a quiet prayer as I closed the lid. I put everything back and went outside.

I found a mechanic's dolly and got under the RV. The guy who designed the vehicle would not have recognized it, especially the wiring.

When I returned to the hidden loft several lights blinked on the security panel and Anson's beeper begged for attention. One of those very expensive two way pagers! Suddenly I realized the RV must have a self-destruct. Anson didn't take many chances!

A horrible suspicion pulled at my insides. Anson could buy anything material he wanted. He could hire just about anything done. He clearly wanted to be an artist, but I'd seen no work of his, complete or in progress. Just a well equipped, but sterile studio.

I had all I needed from Anson for the time being. I wrapped him in artist's canvas and put him next to Marty in his own private morgue. Then I disposed of or hid everything related to blood or violence. Finally I relocked the door to the hidden loft.

Down in the garage again I found a remote control for the big door. I pulled the party transport truck as far in as possible. A few minutes later the door slid closed behind the Imagemaker. I dragged James and Matthew into the van and returned it to the street. Finally I shoved all the party gear into the empty cages as best I could. I locked all the locks, reactivated the alarms, then exited the building through the skylight I came in.

I drove to an isolated house I own and securely locked the crew-cuts in the basement.

The pre-dawn chorus of birds ready for the new day assaulted my ears as I parked outside Doc's high walled clinic grounds. Once inside the treatment building I paged Doc and got an update. Except for the facial damage and a surprisingly light concussion, she checked out physically fine. Mentally…

"Her blood has traces of many of the so called 'recreational chemicals.' Samples of her hair and nails indicate that this has been going on for many months. She must have taken a fairly heavy dose of several things including some hallucinogenics about the time the beatings started."

Doc sighed. He treats many drug users, but he still has trouble comprehending why people do it. "From what little she's said coming out of your gas, I believe much of the torture seems dream like. You know I dislike violence, but I hope you kill whoever did this."

From Dr. Seth Howe Wannamaker that statement flabbergasted me. "Way ahead of you Doc," I said. "Now it looks like I've got to bring him back to life. There's at least one murder involved here. I've got a sinking feeling that's only the beginning. And you'll love this. The person you're so happy to see dead has blood relatives on your Clinic's Blue Ribbon, Blue Blood, Board of Directors."

He stared at me for a moment. To see if I was joking, I guess, then he replied, "Ah, well, I only rely on them as fund raising tools. They rarely have anything to say that hasn't been suggested before by some of my staff, probably an orderly. But, if this causes funding problems… You may need to, (What is the term?) knock over a few more drug dealers to make up the difference."

That's Doc! Work to do and he lets everything else sort itself out. "Doc, I've got a wild idea. You'll have to make some medical decisions quickly. Will she be able to travel in the next couple of days? And could she wear one of my masks and look close to normal?"

Doc blinked a couple of times. I've asked him to do some strange medical things in the last fifteen years or so. This about topped the list. "What, exactly do you want to do?' I told him.

Doc woke me up about two hours later. I'd crashed on his office couch. If he'd brought an unqualified "yes" or "no," I'd have been able to tell. Obviously a great big 'IF' lurked somewhere.

"I have checked all my references, even the new ones in what you call 'on-line.' I have reviewed the transcripts of what she's said. Physically she could travel in one day, preferably two. Her mental state keys on one thing. Her Black Knight. Remember I said most of the beatings seemed dream-like? But, she does remember that they happened. The last few hours are frightfully clear to her. She knows much was done to her face. We have not let her see the damage.

"Apparently she spent the days before the beatings started with a nice enough chap who liked swashbuckler movies. They watched a number of them as she took many pills. She especially remembers seeing

John Borman's "Excalibur." She got taken back to "Ansie." He gave her something to drink. Then she woke tied up as you found her. Before the haze of the pills faded away she kept telling herself that a Black Knight would come to her rescue. All the pills finally wore off and her hope evaporated. She remembers quite vividly the last few blows. Then a mist sprang up and out of it strode her Black Knight who rescued her as she swooned in his arms."

"My combat rig," I said, "and my gas gun. I really hosed the place down."

"To be sure," Doc continued. "She keeps asking about you. She believes that this 'Ansie' is dead. That means safety to her. Even if we told her about you taking 'Ansie's' place, I do not believe she could deal with it. If you walked in as that sub-human creature, I think her mind would implode. We would loose her forever. Right now, 'Black Knight,' she believes in you and only you. You must appear as she remembers you. That is the easy part. Then you must show her, make her understand, how you become 'Ansie.' I will be watching. If you can make her understand, truly understand, then I allow your plan to continue. Step by step, mind you. If she has any problems at all, its off, over, finished! Do I make myself clear."

At about noon Doc escorted Dana into a luxurious treatment suite. I watched a bank of monitors in the next room. Five color TV cameras showed every bit of the room. I could even see most of the props we'd planted there. Doc sat her down in a ten thousand dollar recliner chair that performed many medical functions and made a half decent lie detector and full vitals monitor, to boot. She looked awake but not quite fully alert. The pain killers, I decided. Doc assured her that somebody would be there in a moment and departed.

They had not left her alone before. This was the first test. A full trauma team waited behind a hidden door if they were needed. After a moment she stood and headed for a small mirror that hid one of the cameras. Doc joined me as she looked into it. Her face was sheaved in the thinnest plastic paint-on bandages Doc could manage. Beneath that the outlines of stitches, staples, and a system of tiny wound drains could be seen dimly. Her head had been shaved to patch the cuts that extended beyond her face.

Doc, and the other members of his team, had not sugar-coated her condition. They knew, even with me not involved, she would look at her earliest chance. Well, she looked, and looked, but she did not cry. She slowly turned away and resumed her place in the chair. A few seconds later Doc gave me the go signal. "Her vitals have not jumped as much as I feared."

I waited by the front door to the room for the count of ten. Doc turned on another medical gadget with lots of lights to attract Dana's attention. Next to me ten pounds of Dry Ice bubbled in various containers creating a fog of sorts. When I reached ten I raised the gas gun and stepped into the room. The fog roiled in around me. In just about my normal voice I said, "Hello Dana."

She turned, expecting to see another medical professional. Her eyes widened as she took me in. I wore black no-shine boots, black baggy multi-pocket trousers, a belt full of pouches and holsters, and even baggier black shirt with even more pockets and a shapeless black sniper's veil. "Its good to see you're awake," I continued.

She stared long enough that I started to worry. Then she smiled, or tried to. "I wasn't dreaming," she breathed. "I knew I wasn't dreaming. These people are so kind, but some of them rolled their eyes when I said a Black Knight rescued me."

"Most of them," I said as I holstered the gas gun, "have never seen me. Only Doc Wanamaker knows I'm here. Can we keep it our secret?"

"Anything you say, Mr. Knight. Or is that Sir Knight? Do you have a name?"

"To know my name puts you in more danger. If you had been less injured, I would not have involved Doc directly. How do you feel?"

"I'm mostly numb from the neck up. I ache all over, but the pain killers cover most of that." She paused, then blurted, "You killed Ansie, didn't you? I hope I didn't dream that."

"Yes, Anson, the third, is dead." I saw her visibly relax. "I need to talk to you about Anson, and the shelter. Are you up for that? Good. Doc says you're on a liquid diet today. Some tasty custom made high nutrition milk shakes will be here soon. Now tell me how did you meet Anson?"

At three o'clock we took a break and I talked to Doc. He gave the go ahead to try out the resurrection idea.

"Dana, do you know what a death mask is?" She nodded. I pulled the cover off a rolling table and picked up an object. "This is Anson's. I made it because I often take people's places. Usually when I make one of these the person is alive. You'd see where breathing tubes went in the nostrils. I want you to help me become Anson for awhile. I didn't have a chance to study him. I don't know how he moves, so I need your help. No one else knows he's dead. Only you can give me the information, the critical review of how well I do. I know you won't like seeing me as Anson, but I need to help all the girls at the shelter and the ones who have left. Can you handle that?"

Very quietly, Dana said that she could. For the next hour she saw what only Doc had seen before. I took off my veil. Her smile turned into a frown as I told her that the face of the gas company guy was not my own. Then I took that face off. The base coat of my makeup turned her off. Not surprising, it turns me off too, sometimes. Then I picked up the mask built from Anson's death mask. I let her touch it. For a second, I thought she'd throw it on the floor and stomp it a few times. Finally she grimaced and let go. She watched with mixed emotions as I put it on and cleaned up the edges.

Dana almost freaked out when I changed my vocal implant to the Parker's range. I spent a few minutes showing her different voices. Finally, I called Doc in the next room and got the go ahead for the next step.

"Dana," I began, "would you like to get some second hand revenge against Ansie?"

"Sure!" She paused, then continued, "But isn't it a little bit late for that?"

"Physically, yes. Financially, no. I believe that a lot of women need to be located and helped. I couldn't do that alone if I wanted to. Your medical bills are going to hit six figures. Anson could afford that in a heartbeat. If you're game, you and Anson will run out to Nevada in his fancy RV and get married."

"Married to that..." My she had a mouth. Its a wonder the fire sprinklers didn't go off. Suddenly she bit a word square in half and started laughing. Finally, she got a grip. "I must still be a little punchy," she told me between chuckles. "What you really mean is that I marry that face you're wearing. Of course, I become a widow before I meet his relatives?"

"That's right," I agreed, "and you get your face burned in the same accident. If you're game I'll get started on a temporary mask for you."

I spent the rest of the afternoon working very gently with Dana. I'd found her small purse while cleaning out The Third's studio area. Her driver's license and shelter photo-ID's gave what I needed to create the outside of the mask.

Doc helped and held Dana's hand while I made the mold of what passed for her face. The old boy hit it dead on. Dana would do almost anything for her "Black Knight." When I finally started to leave she said nothing, but clearly showed signs of distress. I put both hands lightly on her shoulders while I told her, "Dana, you are safe. You will be safe. Doc protects his patients like the Secret Service. On any given day there are several faces here that you'd recognize in a heartbeat. But the world never knows that. You are now his patient. The staff will treat you, but they will not know who you are.

"Doc will be your link to me. I have work to do. I'll return as soon as I can. Please be ready to help me then. That means relax as best you can. Rest and start getting well. Can you do that for me? And Doc?"

Dana looked up at me, still in Ansie's face. She blinked a couple of times, then looked away. Finally just a ghost of a smile showed as she turned back. "I'll be good. Just remember, along with everything else you have to buy me an engagement ring."

I told her I would as I left. I think I heard a tiny laugh as the door closed behind me. She knew she'd just startled the heck out of me.

No sleep for me. I called my source for information on the city's upper crust. He gave me the name of a discrete jeweler who made "house calls" and likely dealt with the Anson's from time to time. Using The Third's voice I arranged to meet him in a private room at the metro's most expensive Sushi bar. On the way there in a classic Jaguar borrowed from one of Doc's detox patients, I tested Anson's plastic by buying Dana a set of travel luggage at an upscale leather goods shop.

The sushi proved excellent. Over a second California roll I bought the most expensive ring the jeweler offered that did not actually appear flashy. The Anson way, my source said, value, but never ostentation. Before I headed where I'd stashed the crew-cuts I called a professional shopper. I gave her Dana's sizes with an order for a complete travel wardrobe and sundries be ready for pick-up by noon the next day. Then I requested three outfits for me. Finally I added a request for a stocked liquor travel case including campaign and an ice bucket. I could feel rumors in motion before I hung up.

The crew-cuts turned out to be no help at all. I'd left them in separate, sound proofed rooms in that house's basement. Wearing jackboots, a black S.W.A.T. style tactical uniform, and a black leather mask I got nothing out of them with threats or a little rough stuff. I might have been questioning statues.

Finally I gave that up and gassed both rooms. I strapped them to gurneys. Then I gave them a drug mix that produces twilight sleep. I left them for a few hours with headphones on playing special music. I drove to several places taking care of business that could not wait while I went out of town with Dana.

Back at the house, James and Matthew still listened to the music with its subliminal messages. This long technique ends up making the subject trust a voice they get conditioned to. I set my vocal implant to the proper setting and began. Both gave me the same story. Working at the Shelter for Troubled Women only served as an initiation or test of abilities to join a group they knew only by the code name "Our Brotherhood." What they told me about the group made Ronald Reagan seem like a flaming liberal. They did not know each other before the shelter. James and Matthew were not the names given them at birth. Each only wanted to belong to something bigger than themselves. Our Brotherhood expected them to pass a number of tests before they joined. Turned out both of them believed myearlier interrogation to be simply another of those trials. No wonder I'd talked to the walls. I gave up.

By the time I finished making all of my arrangements the eastern sky glowed with the false dawn. In place of sleep I spent an hour using a technique learned from one of my honorary uncles in the business. I entered a meditative state. My mind disconnected from my body to give it near total rest. For want of a better term I let my left and right brains go their separate ways for a fixed period. The conscious part of me stood back and watched as everything that would have been released by a deep R.E.M. sleep fired itself off. Its sort of like watching a huge fireworks display in black and white and without sound. I arose with a refreshed and clear mind. My body still seemed tired. I hoped to sleep fully the following night.

Doc's clinic serves four star food. I joined Dana for breakfast. I let her direct me as I put Ansie through various situations and physical moves. Telling Ansie what to do and how to do it seemed to amuse her. With Dana's coaching I felt ready to take over the life of William George Edward Anson, the Third. At least his public side. I sure didn't want to bump into any of his relatives or cronies.

I pulled up to the Renaissance Shelter for Troubled Women in another flashy sports car belonging to one of Doc's detox patients. I bid the receptionist the cheerful, but down my nose, greeting that Dana said everybody got, at least in public. I told her I'd wait for Mrs. O'Toole in her office.

With my ears open for approaching footsteps I dug into the files. I'd put about five pounds of stuff in a carry bag when I heard her steps approaching. By the time she opened the door, I'd killed most of the lights, sat down at her desk, placed a mini-gas gun and .38 pistol in easy reach and had my hand on my vocal implant.

She entered quickly, obviously gripping her temper for dear life. "Mister Anson, what are you..."

I raised my hand sharply and she stopped speaking. I began with Anson's voice, "Good Morning, Mrs. O'Toole..." As I paused, I sent the implant to the Twilight Zone. "...Do you have any idea who I really am?"

She looked like somebody had jabbed her with a cattle prod. She almost lost it, then pulled herself together. Pretty good recovery. I've seen big time hoods freak completely at the sound of The Voice.

"Yes, I believe I might know. Why are you here?"

"To find the truth. Some might call me The Voice of Truth. You are either a scientist with fewer scruples than the original Victor Frankenstein, or you are in way over your head. Possibly there is another answer. What is the truth, Mrs. O'Toole?"

I let her gather herself, but I watched like a hawk. I expected a bluff, at first. That's not what I got. She didn't move much, but her wound like a spring body actually relaxed. A tiny look of relief flickered across her face. If she had intended for me to see such a look it would have been much broader.

"I've heard whispers about you and what you do," she began, "If those whispers are correct, I need your help to protect the girls."

I chuckled a bit. When I do that in The Voice, its not pretty. "Protect them, from you, perhaps."

"No! When I'm left alone I help those young women."

I put real steel in my words. "How? By feeding them drugs? Tell me how that helps them."

"Because I have the secret to changing their lives." Fire burned in her eyes. "You've heard of the cycle of dependence? These girls are not the casual users who need detoxification and some counseling. They've all had that more than once, then gone right back to their self-destructive ways.

"About sixty years ago my father worked at a secret facility that reprogrammed people. He helped develop an aversion therapy drug. He never knew the rest of the system, no one did. When the center closed he managed to recreate his work. But the drug alone was not enough. Do you follow me?"

I took a shot in the dark. "That center was located near..." I named a town in upstate New York. She caught her breath, coming even closer to losing it than before. "This is not the first time part of that technology has surfaced," I added.

"Then you know how powerful the effects can be. I studied my father's notes, but the only way I had of successfully treating someone meant using the drug and hypnosis right after the undesirable behavior. My teen-aged daughter all but killed herself with drugs. I planted a homing device on her and forcibly treated her after each drug spree. She never understood and still hates me, but she's been drug free for ten years.

"Once I tried to interest a pharmaceutical house in my work. They threw me out citing potential liability. The Ansons hold directorships on that company's board. Sometime later their agents found me and demanded that I treat William, the Third's, rebellious younger brother. They offered lots of research money if I did, and tabloid headlines and possible misconduct charges if I did not. I learned a lot more treating Thornton Anson. They insisted I not only treat his addiction, but remove all his other undesirable behaviors. He ended up an amiable zombie, with no will of his own.

"The elder members of the family kept their word and set me up in this place. That's when William, the Third, shoved his way in. In addition to the ones I wanted to treat, he'd add special girls. If I didn't like that he'd tell the authorities I'd deliberately overdosed his brother and misrepresent my work. Where he gets those automaton security guards, I do not know. A new pair arrives about every six months. They do as he says, but to my eye, they despise him. William sees that they keep me on a very short leash.

"The young women I've treated without interference have all, every one, gone on to a normal life. Some I still hear from, some I do not. William places the special ones himself. "

That seemed to be about the end of the story. Then somebody kicked in the door.

# part 3

# Getting Out Of Town, In One Piece

September 21, 1989

There must have been one local good ol' boy in the squad. I figured I'd done a pretty good job of leaving no trail. Still they came on. I kept the few rounds in the beat up Model 1911 Colt for a last resort. The character I'd taken it from would not be wanting the weapon anytime soon. If ever.

We kept climbing. We'd come to a nearly shear cliff. About a quarter mile further on a series of splits in the rock created a couple of natural switchbacks. I could not tell if there was any place to go once we reached the top. I hurried Dana up the first rough ramp, then about half way up the second. A lot of boulders in this area provided cover.

In addition the the gun, knife, and parachute cord I'd taken from our former guard, I now carried a couple of straight and strong pieces of wood about six feet long. I surveyed the free standing boulders and the cracks in the cliff edge. I knew I only had a short time to put together an ambush.

As I swept my gaze around once more the look in Dana's eyes froze me. No fear, no dread, no resignation, either

She smiled as much as her mask and facial dressings allowed, "Its time to fight them, isn't it?"

Somewhere on that mountainside I'd lost a liability and gained an asset. Suddenly I was not *quite* as sorry I'd gotten her into this.


September 18, 1989

Somebody put a huge amount of force behind that old solid wood door. The latch snapped and slammed the door's edge directly into Mrs. O'Toole left shoulder blade. The impact threw her forward. She sprawled over a heavy wood office chair. I heard her land on the floor like a sack of sand.

The door rebounded from the impact. A ham-like hand pushed it back open. In stepped someone who could have been James or Matthew's older brother. Or maybe father. The short cut sandy hair and blue eyes with a bull neck made me think of an Aryan recruiting poster. "Uncle Adolph Wants You!" He wore a well cut suit that fit him fairly decently, but a uniform would suit him better. Any uniform.

My mind raced. He held no weapon, but his right hand kept his jacket pushed aside just like the first part of the F.B.I. draw for a pistol in the small of the back. He might even be a cop of some kind. I doubted it. On his own turf Anson would have gone ballistic over an intrusion. This was not his turf, at least technically. I kept his face frozen.

All that flashed through my mind in the second or so before he spoke, "Where are they?"

I made Anson look like his control teetered on the edge. "Where are whom, my friend?"

"Don't get coy with me, Anson," he replied evenly. "James and Matthew didn't check in at the assigned time. Where are they?"

Oh, brother, or maybe brotherhood, I thought. Those wind-up-toy thugs are on that short of a leash? My questioning of them never went in that direction. Apparently this character represented the Rent-A-Thug service. Dana told me that Anson said the word "friend" to a lot of people. Especially ones who would never think of him in that manner. I tossed it out again for the reaction I might get. "Friend, I have not seen them since I was last at the Shelter. I did talk with someone who was their guest last night. He says they ran the group back where they came from and departed. I just assumed they decided to sleep a little late this morning."

"Not only did they not check in, they do not answer their pagers," he spat out like he tasted something unpleasant.

"Well, then, let us check their quarters," I had Anson tell him with a false cheery voice. "But first let me check on Mrs. O'Toole."

"She can wait."

"Perhaps she can, as far as a doctor is concerned. But if she wakes up? All she will know is that she was hit from behind. And that I'm missing. She calls for help for herself. My name gets mentioned. Instant police and media circus. Do you want that? I didn't think so."

Mrs. O'Toole turned out to be playing possum. She might have a couple of cracked ribs, but I found no other broken bones. As I carefully rolled her over she winked at me. I made a show of putting a cushion under her head. She "woke up" when my lips silently told her to.

"Mrs. O'Toole, we are so sorry. My friend tripped as he was about to knock. The door slammed into you. You just rest here for a moment. I'll call in a nice friendly doctor to make sure you are not seriously injured. Can you do that for me?"

A few moments later Anson's unnamed friend and I climbed up to the crew-cuts quarters. They lived in the only part of the complex with four stories. Above the third floor was "no woman's land."

How could I take the guy out? This character would be ready for any kind of fighting the real Anson was equipped for. Then I remembered that my society expert told me that Anson competed in college gymnastics as an underclassman and did the Decathlon as a senior.

Fifteen steps led from the third floor to the fourth. I took note of a tear in the carpet runner on the twelfth tread. With seemingly renewed energy I bounded up the flight two stairs at a time. I heard supervisor thug pick up his pace, as well.

Then I put my foot directly into that breach in the carpet. Anson began a forward body pitch. Flailing arms missed a grip on the bannister, pushing off, instead. Anson's body spun around. At that point I slipped my foot out of the carpet to literally dive at the man desperately trying to slow down behind me.

I tucked into a compact ball as I slammed into his midsection just as hard as I could manage. Together we headed back down to the landing. His head made a dent in the lathed plaster wall. Most of the rest of him bounced a bit off of the landing floor.

I picked myself up with a look of astonishment on Anson's face. Not needed. Out cold, whoever he was. I cataloged my newly acquired bumps and bruises while I searched him.

"Thomas Howard" read his driver's license from two states over. Didn't believe that for a second. Two slightly used credit cards in the same name. Receipt for a large tank of gas and coffee at a truck stop on the west side of town. Eighty-seven dollars in well used bills. And tucked away, two super crisp one hundreds. Keys that looked like they fit a Ford F-150 truck. I pocketed his wallet as a gaggle of girls opened the stairwell door.

I explained the "accident" to them as James and Mathew's "uncle" catching his foot on the carpet behind me. I asked that they call an ambulance while I sought identification of the "uncle" in his vehicle. I found the proper F-150 parked out of sight with a fast retreat in mind. I moved it two blocks over. Passing my own vehicle I snatched up a few things. Back on the landing I palmed an auto-injector containing a nearly undetectable sleeping compound. As I felt around for broken bones I injected him high in the inner thigh. Mr. "Howard" would not likely wake up for a week.

Paramedics packed Uncle John Doe off to the hospital while I answered some questions from the police who arrived soon after.

Later on I told Mrs. O'Toole to expect visitors who would both protect her and check out her work. Before I drove off in Mr. Howard's truck I called my old buddy Curt Van Loan of Havens International Media to get the very quiet investigation started. Once he understood to origin of Mrs. O'Toole work, he couldn't get things moving fast enough.

Doc Wanamaker's extremely expensive, but low key Cadillac town car pulled up to the most expensive Northern Italian restaurant in the city. The liveried chauffeur hurried to open the rear passenger door before the bistro's doorman arrived. I beat them both by bounding from behind the decorative planting.

"Sorry, friends," I said as I slipped them each a twenty dollar bill. "This time, I will do the honors."

I pulled the door open with a flourish. Just as we practiced, Dana took my hand to get out of the car. She looked mysteriously and understatedly stunning in a cocktail dress with matching hat and stiff traditional veil. Sort of like Audrey Hepburn in *Breakfast At Tiffiney's*. I made a great show of kissing her hand. She laughed as arm in arm we made our way to a private dining room. When we left she wore the ring. I insisted that she walk as if nothing had changed. Conservative setting, or not, that rock would be noticed.

Later, in the flashy top down sports car, I drove the two of us past a number of places frequented by the upper crust. Finally I drove into a public garage where we switched to a VW Beetle with tinted windows. Soon after we boarded Anson's RV and headed west.

After three hours of driving I concluded nobody followed us. I checked us in at the next RV park I found. After the excitement of our in-town antics wore off Dana had gone silent on me. She'd been staring off into the darkness from the passenger's captain's chair for quite some time. I was beginning to be concerned. She continued to stare through the windshield until I blocked the view with the RV's sliding curtains. She blinked a couple of times, then began staring at her hands.

"Are you feeling okay, Dana?" I asked.

"Yes, I am," she replied with a bit of a surprised look. "After we left all the city lights behind I got a bit bored. Then I realized I hadn't popped any kind of happy pill for days. Doc Wanamaker even reduced my pain medication quite a bit. So I waited for the urge to take something. But it didn't come. It didn't come. I managed to pocket a few things at the clinic. Just in case. But I don't want them. At least not yet."

"I'm glad to hear that," I replied. I neglected to tell her that her "stash" contained only sugar or mild caffeine pills Doc's staff left out for her to pilfer. "Now, do you think you can sleep?"

"Only if you share the bed with me," she replied demurely. "There! That sent your eyebrows up. Oh don't worry. I'm not going to attack you. I'll sleep better with someone I trust within reach. And, Sir Black Knight, I'm not about to let you be chivalrous and sleep on the floor, or in a chair. You sleep on the floor, I'll sleep on the floor. End of story."

Well, that settled that. Just before we turned out the lights Dana commented at some of the scars now visible on my body, "I guess being a Knight Errant has its hazards. What happened there?"

"Drug wholesaler with a K-Bar fighting knife," I answered absently. At the same time I wondered how badly she'd freak-out if I told her that she was sitting almost directly above Anson, the Third's, belly button in the RV's secret morgue. When she settled herself I slid in on the other side of the queen sized mattress, as far from her as possible. I began working on Uncle Kent's mental trick to fall asleep nearly instantly.

Then Dana said with a low chuckle, "There's one good reason, a tactical reason you might say, to leave you alone tonight. You need to save it for the wedding night. There's no way in Hell Ansie would spend his wedding night in any RV. Anyway, the honeymoon suite aftermath had better look Homeric."

I managed to get to sleep just over an hour later.

The following morning I fixed breakfast for the two of us. Doc's kitchen sent along a bunch of good for you but easy to digest food. I ran Dana's portions through one of those hand held baby food mills. Serious chewing would be out of the question for her for some time.

As she sipped an orange juice with banana puree I asked, "Can you tell me why Anson turned on you? It might help my impersonation."

"That's easy. I just didn't realize it at the time. I never felt comfortable with those, I guess you'd say, 'Asianized' eyes. They bugged me. My last assignment for Ansie was babysitting a computer programming genius. He told me that once he saw the project's solution he wouldn't know, or care, if I was there or not. So, courage built up by happy pills, I snuck out to the plastic surgeon's office. He pulled the sutures changing my eyes' shape. Two days later I put the programmer in the limo to the airport and went to Ansie's studio. He gave me a couple of supposed happy pills and a Virgin Mary to wash them down. I woke up like you found me. You know the rest."

We spent the rest of the day traveling west, like tourists. Tourists who were head over heels in love. That's a tough sell when the couple can't "suck face" in public. We would almost kiss. Then Dana'd pretend shyness. Then, hand in hand, we'd retreat to the RV. We giggled a lot.

Gunsight, Colorado, near the pass and park of the same name, turned out to be part pleasant tourist haven and part destination center for people who live for many miles around. The law offices of James W. Billings, Esquire, turned out to be in the detached former garage of his residence just off the main drag.

I made a point of keeping the RV away from that area. I sure as Hell didn't want him connecting Anson with the burglary coming soon to his office. I signed us in at a K.O.A. overlooking the town. We spent the rest of the afternoon walking the trails around the place, hand in hand.

Come full dark, Dana watched me put on the gas company guy's face.

"Now that's a face I'd be willing to kiss," she told me. "If I could, that is. But, do you really need that entire arsenal?"

Her eyes had grown a bit wider as I filled every pocket of my dark outfit with tools, camera, gas gun, and a .32 automatic. The two throwing knives up my jacket sleeves proved a bit much for her.

"In my business you tend to be a belt and suspenders type of person. Pack everything just in case. Ideally, Billings, Esquire, will have a small town mentality and all I'll need is a credit card for the front door. But, even if he only has a friendly dog, I may need the gas gun. And so on…

"Now, we paid extra for the cable TV connection. Keep the sound to a reasonable level, try to laugh at any funny parts, but don't wait up for me."

"I'll do my best," she replied hesitantly. She slipped her arms around me and squeezed. I could feel her body trembling slightly. Then she giggled a bit, "A knight who works at night. A knight's night's work. Have a good night, Sir Knight."

Impulsively, her mask covered lips barely brushed my cheek. She recoiled, as her eyes teared up like faucets. I spent the next twenty minutes comforting her. When she regained some control I showed her one method for reducing pain without drugs. I finally slipped out as she began to practice Uncle Jethro's technique.

Between all the maps I'd grabbed that day and our scouting walks in the afternoon, I knew I could cut the nearly five miles by road to

Billings' place to just over one on foot. And what a beautiful night for a "stroll."

Less than an hour later I came over the mouthpiece's back fence. No apparent dogs, and a steady stream of music from the house on a radio station that seemed to be in love with John Denver. I wondered if James W. might be getting a little "Rocky Mountain High," himself.

I needed more that a credit card to get in. Top of the line locks on both front and back doors. No monitored alarm system, but a speaker big enough to wake the dead, if activated. I wondered if the alarm played John Denver, too.

Finally, I got in. Using an infrared flashlight and goggles I searched Billings' filing cabinet. Anson's file turned out to be fairly thick. Under one of those micro-thin "space blankets" to block the light I photocopied the whole thing. That took longer than I intended. The moon edged over the peaks as I departed.

A lot later than I'd hoped I arrived back at Anson's RV. From outside I could just hear George Carlin holding forth on the weirdness of the English language. I waited for a punch line. I smiled as I heard Dana's slight laugh. I gave the all clear signal and entered. To my surprise she still sat as I'd left her, in the Lotus Position.

"Welcome, Sir Knight," she breathed. "Help me get up. I think my joints are frozen in place."

With a chuckle I assisted her to her feet. Carefully I moved a few strands of her wig away from her eyes. And with George Carlin still trying to to tickle our funny bones, I spread the table and counter with photocopies.

Billings had not billed Anson for all that many hours of service. But his hourly rate would have astonished the average solicitor back home. When your client operates under an assumed name, I guess the sky's the limit.

The relationship started several years before. First some title searches for properties in the region. Next Billings arranged proxy buyers for a few of the land parcels. In one case, after the sale, he retrieved mineral rights sold by the previous owner.

Dana and I started to mark the plots on the set of Colorado survey maps I'd brought along. Turned out we only needed two. Some were on the east edge of one map. The rest were on the west edge of the next map. With the exception of a small wedge of land, Anson, through Billings, controlled an entire mountain. And, in conjunction with something called Alliance Properties, Billings fought all forms of development anywhere near the mountain.

Then we looked at the fuel bills. One bill a month. Not for propane, but for old fashioned fuel oil. Deliveries from two different companies, in two separate towns, to two different locations. The even month bills varied by as much as thirty per cent. The odd numbered months' bills were oddly the same. Varied by no more than three per cent. We went back to the maps. Both locations ended up being on the same survey map. About a quarter mile apart as the crow flies. A high altitude crow, that is. The ridge leading to the top of Anson's mountain separated the two. I estimated the road distance between them at well over five miles.

As we prepared to sleep I resumed wearing Ansie's face. With a final rub around the seams I remarked, "What can be so different about two slopes on the same mountain flank?"

"Just like you, Ansie," replied Dana, with an ironic chuckle. "You/He never wanted his right hand to know what his left was doing. His family's companies never knew a thing about the 'special' services I arranged or provided to their out of town visitors. Anything to keep them happy and productive."

With that she took off her wig. Then she carefully slipped the back of her head into the padded brace that kept her face from touching anything. When she settled in I joined her. Hesitantly, she sought out my hand.

"Thank you, Sir Knight," she breathed, "for everything."

We fell asleep with our fingers still touching.

The next morning we headed off to see where all that fuel oil went. After about thirty miles of winding roads and beautiful views we found a fenced off area marked "Western Ridge Cooperative." The place consisted of three buildings and a few small sheds surrounded by a high chain link fence. And all of it was old. Including the artificially flat area that used to be part of the mountain's side. I guesstimated that the blasting and one building dated back to the 1930's. The rest seemed to be from the fifties and sixties. The fence obviously being the newest of all.

I pulled the RV to the side of the road. Carrying with me an air of disgust, I proceeded to check the rolling love nest's tires. Behind the tinted windows Dana snapped a few Polaroid pictures. Two miles down the road I pulled the RV into a State Rest Area.

"That seemed to be a dead end," said Dana, "unless you saw things I didn't."

"I think that's what we're supposed to think. Those commercial gas and fuel oil pumps haven't been touched in a bunch of years. However, fuel oil deliveries take place outside the locked fence. But the gate's been opened, now and then. The only disturbances in the rocks and weeds lead to the old service station that's right against the rock wall. The one service door is tall enough to accommodate this vehicle."

I fired up the engine saying, "We'll take a quick look at the other place, then run off and get married."

"Is that all you're going to do?" Dana asked.

"For the moment, yes. Doc wants you back in his care. The sooner the better. When Anson is officially dead I'm headed back here. But, when I go over that fence I want to be loaded for bear. You know how devious and unprincipled Anson was. For all we know he's been boarding Dr. Frankenstein and his latest monster back there."

Dana chuckled at that. I didn't try to dissuade her that I really wasn't joking. Some of the things my dad and my honorary uncles encountered back in the day, well…

Three miles later we began to see small signs for the "Fork In The Road Cafe." Then, right there, at the fork in the state roads, it stood, along with a gas station. I pulled in, topped off the gas, and put some air in the tires. As I was settling up with the friendly attendant Dana stuck her head out.

Smiling as much as her makeup permitted she called, "Ansie, I'm thirsty. Why don't we get some of those hand dipped shakes that sign raves about?"

As it turned out that was about the best idea either one of us had that day. Those milkshakes were delicious and ended up having additional benefits. Bea, the combination manager, cook, and soda jerk, chatted with us as she worked. As she began cooking burgers to go, I asked about the Western Ridge Cooperative property.

"With that beautiful view, seems like somebody ought to put up a motel or attraction there."

"Honey, you aren't the first person with that notion. But that land and stuff's tied up with Chief Hanks' estate."

"Chief? Indian chief?" I asked.

"Nope, honey. Navy Chief Petty Officer. Retired and got about as far away from the ocean as a body can. Ran the gas station 'n' souvenir shop. Lived above it, from the late fifties. Hated his first name of Fletcher. So everybody called him Chief. Really nice fellow, 'cept he seemed to be expecting World War Three any old time.

"He passed on ten, twelve, years ago. Later, some of his family tried puttin' together that Cooperative deal. Only lasted a year or so. Then the fence went up. Shame that. Used to drive up there to watch the sunset."

Back in the RV Dana alternated grinding her food with feeding me as I drove. Then we came around a pretty sharp curve cut into the mountain slope. Across the valley, canyon really, I spotted a large natural terrace. Any number of trees grew on it. But they couldn't come close to hiding a bunch of frame buildings and Quonset huts. The terrace was wide enough that the road didn't hug the edge, but seemed to lie about one third of the way toward the main slope.

When we reached the terrace I pulled the RV onto the shoulder away from the buildings. I got out and checked the tires away from the compound. Then I stretched as I made my way to the other side. I checked the rear tire.

As I headed for the front tire a man with a pump action shotgun appeared in front of me. Behind me came the sound of a shotgun shell being chambered. I'd been mousetrapped by experts.

I kept my body still as I took the briefest of glances to the rear. I won't repeat what I thought to myself as I realized that these two men could be pod-brothers of James and Matthew.

Then all doubt went out the window as the man in front said, "Okay, Anson. The Colonel wants to see you. Right now."

Then he pulled a thermal imaging device from behind his back. Raising his voice he called, "Whoever you are in the vehicle. Come out now. Real slowly."

I was not rigged for combat in any way, shape, or form, except for my teeth. I cursed myself for overconfidence as the remote release let the RV's door swing open. The two men moved to where they had the door in a deadly crossfire. Then, at its sweetest, Dana's voice floated out.

"Be right with you handsome. Just let me finish powdering my nose."

I think all three of our mouths popped open. For different reasons none of us expected this response.

A moment later Dana came down the RV's steps. But this was not quite the Dana I'd seen such a short time ago. Sensible sneakers replaced her airy sandals. Her jeans were turned up because they now rode much, much lower on her hips. Her blouse had been unbuttoned and tied in a fashionable knot around the space between her bra cups. Said cups seemed to be straining to confine more volume than previously.

Somehow I managed not to let my face show the astonishment I felt. Just barely.

Frick and Frack marched us across the road and into the compound without further comment. Other than the two shotguns I saw no weapons, but the place still had a (para)military feel to it. I counted six more men doing various jobs consistent with that. The place was spick and span with some fresh paint and raked leaves. The buildings were old. World War Two surplus, possibly. Two of the Quonset huts' ends were built flush with the natural rock. As I had guessed we headed towards the only all wood, and only two story, building. Headquarters.

Once inside they led us through a typical military orderly room manned my three more pod-brothers. They stopped at a door marked simply "Command."

"Mr. Anson, and friend," announced one of our escorts, after knocking.

A strong voice answered, "Frisk them, and send them in."

My frisking produced Anson's own combination cigar clipper and pen-knife. That brought a look contempt as a "weapon." In the meantime, the other fellow actually blushed a bit and apologized before giving Dana a very light pat down. Then they opened the door and shoved us inside.

I stumbled a bit more than necessary going in. That got me a fuller view of the Colonel's office. The corner room had windows in two walls and a private door. One of the windows and the door pointed through a notch in the trees giving a beautiful view of other mountains in the distance. In a locked Lexan display case between them sat an AK-47 assault rifle with a custom carved red, white, and blue stock. The other two walls were mostly covered by maps and briefing charts. The sole occupant pulled a Colorado map over a building diagram of some kind as we found our footing. I tried to retain the layout for later review.

This Colonel seemed the mold for all the younger pod-brothers. An inch or two taller than me with a slightly heavier build, he wore a crewcut with the crew moderately receding. He looked at Anson/me with distrust. His eyes gave Dana the once over. Somehow I got the impression that he approved of her practical sneakers, but not so much her general provocative appearance. Then he speared me with a look that probably scared most people.

"What's with the sneaking around, Anson?" he rumbled. "Didn't have the nerve to drive right in?"

"The sneaking was for your benefit, friend," I replied. "Just in case you had visitors. We don't want our connection spread around, do we? Especially with potential problems in my home area."

"With three members missing, you might have a point. What can you tell me about that?"

"I've no idea where James and Matthew are." That was true enough. I'd arranged for them to be moved out of town. "As for 'Thomas Howard,'" I continued, "he was a John Doe at Memorial Hospital when I pulled out of town."

"How in blazes did that happen?" asked the Colonel with the implication that my answer had better be good.

"Head injury. His own over-eagerness caused it. He charged up the stairs to James and Matthew's quarters in the Shelter like it was San Juan Hill. Caught his foot in a torn stair runner. Took us both back down." I pulled up one sleeve to show off a bruised area. "I lifted his identification for fear it would not hold up. He's supposed to be the boys' uncle. As soon as I could wrap things up in town I headed out here to consult."

"And I suppose you brought her out as a peace offering," he said with a lear. "Are you supposed to make everything all right for us, young lady?"

"Why not, Colonel?" came Dana's reply. "Especially if you've got real men here. I'm sick of the crowd Ansie pretends to be friends with." She then launched into a laundry list of those friends' sexual shortcomings and perversions. I never want to know how much of that list was real and how much Dana made up.

While she spoke I watched the Colonel's face like a hawk. I'd already noted some probable plastic surgery traces on his face. I invoked my Uncles Jethro and Kent's speedy methods of facial comparison. I limited the possibilities to right wingers and cult leaders. Then a face with a potential match to the plastic markers popped up. And a picture from a New York Clarion article. A picture of a man holding an AK-47. Only a small part of the stock showed, but it matched the one in the room too closely. Colonel George Throckmorton, self-appointed. When threatened, he disappeared, leaving few witnesses, and no living women.

Dana finished her tirade about Ansie's rich buddies, then asked, "How many real men have you got here, Colonel? Ten? Fifteen? Twenty?"

She stepped over and leaned against his desk. "And do I start at the bottom? Or here, at the top?"

The Colonel threw out a smile that would curdle pasteurized milk. He reached for a button by his phone. That's when I vaulted over the desk.

I could have speared him with both feet and slammed him into the wall. But I wanted to keep things relatively quiet. No more than as if he was slapping Anson around. One foot took him in the groin area. As he reflexively bent over I jabbed him in the throat with a knife hand strike.

Out of the corner of my eye I saw Dana grab the stapler off the desk while desperately digging into her bra with the other hand. I lowered the gasping Colonel to the floor. Hastily searching the desk drawers, I soon stuffed a shoe shine rag down his throat. I cinched his arms together with his own web trouser belt.

I changed my vocal implant to the Colonel's range. Then I noticed Dana offering me two objects. Now I knew the secret of her push-up bra. Two of my bombs. One containing my dad's knockout gas. The other, well, very explosive for its size.

"Thanks, Dana," I whispered as I tried to match the Colonel's voice. I snatched the devices from her hands. Then somebody rapped on the door.

"Are you all right, sir?"

"No trouble," I replied in a fair version of his voice. "Mr. Anson just tripped and fell."

My impersonation may not have been good enough. More likely I didn't respond with a proper duress code. Whichever, the door flew open.

As our two escorts charged in I pitched the gas bomb as far as I could into the orderly room. I smashed one of the Colonel's uncomfortable World War Two era hardwood visitor's chairs over the first man's head. The second one leaped into a flying side kick. And a pretty good one, if I had stayed put. Instead, I ducked under him. I grabbed the back of his belt and yanked downward.

His spine probably compressed half an inch with the impact. My open palm then slammed into his face. His head bounced off the floor with a loud thump.

I snatched the heavy letter opener from the desk. Holding my breath I bounded into the Orderly Room. The two men in the back of the room finished folding up right about then. They'd been closest to the gas bomb. The reflexive gasp produced by the first whiff of the gas got them.

The third man, the one near the office door, stumbled toward a fire alarm box on the wall. I knew he would pull the thing before passing out. I threw the letter opener with all my strength. The dull point took him in the back of the clutching hand. The thing barely broke the skin, but the momentum was enough. Reflex jerked the hand away from the alarm. Then he slid down the wall. Out cold.

The compound seemed quiet, but I could not be sure no alarm had been given. I pounced on the two shotguns leaning against the wall. Then I headed back to the office.

Dana still stood in the same position. Her eyes seemed glazed.

"Dana, are you hurt?"

She shook her head, as if to clear it. "Sex games and verbal vendettas I can handle. Brawling, not so much. Sorry."

"Don't be sorry," I replied as I tried to jimmy the AK-47 out of the presentation case. "You helped save the day. Now we need to get out of here. Quick. If the Colonel's who I think he is, we've still got big problems."

Then I did something wrong. The metal rack holding the assault rifle suddenly slid backward into the wall. A second later it dropped from sight.

I muttered a couple of evil words in Vietnamese. "Come on, Dana, we've got to get out of here."

I peered carefully out the window next to the private door. At the bottom of three steps stood a man obviously on guard. In addition to the common unmarked fatigues, he wore an all-in-one webbed pistol belt with magazines, extra pouches, and a Army Colt .45 automatic. The belt would be handed from guard to guard.

Quickly I pulled Dana back a ways from the window. Then I gave her instructions in the simplest and most forceful way I could think of.

"I'm going to tackle the guard standing outside. See that crooked pine tree on the edge of the cleared area? Good. As soon as the guard is on the ground you run for that tree. Get behind it. Look for the RV. If it has been moved keep going in the same direction as the tree. I will catch up. Now, stand by the door. Good. Quietly turn the knob. Now yank it open."

The guard apparently heard the door as it opened. He began to turn like he expected to salute the Colonel. He managed a quarter turn before I flew into him like a javelin. About a second after we hit the ground I saw Dana's sneakers flash by.

I made sure the guard was out cold. I grabbed the pistol belt and a knife he carried. Then I reached back inside for the shotguns. As I surveyed the scene I caught a glimpse of Dana headed further into the wooded slope. I made sure both shotguns had rounds in the chambers. Then I looked around for the rush of troops I knew was coming.

Part 4

# Sculpture, Atomic Piles, And Other Dirty Laundry

September 21, 1989

With Dana's help I'd finished the preparations for the ambush of "Colonel" Throckmorton's troops. They were already trying to verify that we had come up this winding set of ledges. If they thought they had us treed they might just make camp for the night. That was fine by me. The ball of parachute cord in the sentry's pistol belt meant I could surprise them from above, if need be.

I had two rather large bounders ready to roll. One going down the slope we'd climbed. The other should, I prayed, drop straight down on the switchback below.

Dana seemed, well, almost happy. As soon as she finished a task I gave her, she asked for another. Eventually I realized that she was glad to finally be able to do something for me. Up to now she'd pretty much been along for the ride. First, I'd saved her life back in my home town. Then I made sure she received outstanding medical care. Finally, I'd included her on a seemingly safe financial snipe hunt to get back at the estate of the man who turned her face into hamburger. Now she assisted in preparing to fight for our very lives against some of that rich young lunatic's allies.

Quite a change from earlier in the day when the two of us hightailed it out of Throckmorton's Rocky Mountainside compound.

Earlier, The Same Day

Behind the two story frame orderly room building I saw Dana disappear, as instructed, into the woods covering much of the huge natural ledge about halfway up the Colorado mountain. I listened for action from the other six to nine men in the compound. I blessed Dana for unknowingly getting the approximate number of troops out of the Colonel. He'd barely reacted when she mentioned the number fifteen. But he'd reacted not at all to ten or twenty. And I'd put seven at least temporarily out of action. That was just enough for planning purposes.

I heard a couple of unintelligible phrases from the direction where three men had been pulling maintenance on some vehicles. A door slammed in the direction of the Quonset hut that abutted the mountainside beyond it. Then two men in unmarked fatigues loped around another hut headed in my direction. They carried wrenches like clubs.

Without showing a weapon I looked around the corner of the building far enough to be sure of being seen. One of them pointed a wrench at me and the two sped up.

So far I'd seen nothing illegal in the compound. In theory, these two could be simply protecting the legal interests of their employer. I'd better not kill them, I decided. I grabbed one of the two perfectly legal appearing shotguns I'd appropriated. I stepped from cover and fired a round at their legs.

With the two running side by side, one round was enough. Both of them took a number of pellets in a leg. Probably in both legs. Not fatal. Probably no long term damage. But, no more running, for some time.

As the echoes of the shell died away I heard a door crash open onto the hollow metal of a Quonset hut wall. Two seconds later three more of the pod-brothers raced into sight. Now I knew for certain that the gloves were off. Each one carried an Ingram MAC-10 machine pistol fitted with its huge silencer.

One man triggered off a burst at nearly twice the weapon's effective range. I ducked back behind the frame headquarters building. Slugs hit the ground in front of where I stood. Others broke several orderly room windows.

They were still beyond the extreme effective range of the shotgun when I stepped into view. I lofted two charges of whatever the thing held at them. They jumped up and down as they scattered. Those pellets probably hurt like blue blazes. But no serious damage would result.

I pumped the shotgun. Empty. Plugged for three shells. Street legal just about anywhere. Only the illegal stuff had been kept under cover. I smashed both weapons against the corner of the building. Then I sprinted after Dana, heading for the tall timber.

I found Dana clinging to the far side of a tree about eight-hundred yards from the compound. With a finger to my lips I stopped beside her. She immediately transferred her grip from the tree to me. I could feel her her whole body quivering. Somehow, she managed to hang on to her ironic sense of humor.

"If this is what it means being a Black Knight, I think I'd better settle for being a Lady In Waiting. Thank goodness for that milkshake. I don't think I'd have made it this far without it. I don't suppose you managed to do in the whole bunch?"

"Not hardly," I replied while my mind raced. We needed to keep moving. I had hiked and climbed in the Rockies as a teenager, but I didn't know this particular area from Central Park in New York. I came to a decision. A dangerous one. From the waist-band of Anson's trousers I produced a tiny plastic container. It contained two pills.

"Dana, I should never have come here with you. We should have just gone to Nevada and got married. Now, we're in serious trouble and you simply don't have much physical reserve. I could try to find a hiding spot for us, but there will be enough of them to surround us. And some will have automatic weapons. I could also hide you and draw them off..." That's as far as I got. Her body went as rigid as a statue in my arms.

"No!" she whispered. "No. I can't be alone. I'd fall apart. Isn't there another option?"

"There is. But its the last thing you need. Doc Wanamaker will probably kick my butt between my shoulder blades for even suggesting it." I shook one of the pills into my hand. "This is what I call a Wanamaker's Waker. It gives you energy and keeps you awake. But Doc brews these just for me. For my body, which weighs a lot more than yours. I loose five to ten pounds every time I take one. And when the energy part runs out I can't sleep for at least another six hours. Sometimes a lot more. If you take this, it might just kill you..."

Dana moved with amazing speed. Suddenly my hand was empty. A second later she swallowed hard. "If it kills me, it kills me. Then you won't die trying to protect a helpless piece of street trash. Now, what are we going to do. And how long does this brand of speed take to kick in."

Five minutes later I almost tossed Dana behind a fallen log. We'd begun a steady climb. I figured heading over the ridge held our best chance of survival. Assuming Dana could make it. Then I heard something coming through the trees and bushes behind us.

"Company," I whispered. I slithered to the other end of the

twenty-five foot tree trunk. Signaling Dana to keep her head down I checked the guard's .45.

Vulcan, God of the Forge, and weapon maker extraordinary, was probably laughing his apron off as I made sure a round was chambered. The Colt would pass any inspection for proper cleaning. But the gun felt, well, rickety. Passed from guard to guard, only old Vulcan knew the last time it had been fired. I saw similar weapons in the Army. Intended to hold a prisoner at five or ten paces, not target shooting. Much less combat.

Matt Helm probably would have taken a practice shot at a tree. But, I couldn't alert whoever approached. I peered around the root end of the log. Through the dangling, muddy roots I could see signs of movement. I prepared to fire.

The first round should tell me one or two things. First: could I hit the board side of a barn with the thing. Second, if I managed to hit someone: would they take care of their wounded. If they did, that lessened the odds against us. If they didn't, I'd better shoot only to kill. I waited.

Then three crewcut city pod-brothers came into view. They wore web-belts with ammo and first aid pouches. They carried MAC-10's. They looked determined, but obviously lacked combat training. Their eyes swept the ground for footprints. But none of the three scanned the whole area for danger. They saw something on the ground. Then they headed for about the middle of the log. Side by side.

I squeezed off a round aiming for the left thigh of the center man. At about forty feet I hit the guy on the right above the knee. He yelled and went down.

Suddenly the air was full of bullets. Some came in my general direction, but not many. When the two MAC's ran dry I stood up. As they fumbled for fresh magazines I threw most of the Model 1911's load at them. I aimed for the center of mass and prayed. My third round took one in the armpit. He spun to the ground. Then the third pod-brother showed some brains under fire. He dropped his weapon to snatch up the unfired one from the ground. Clumps of dirt flew as he walked the line of fire towards me. In the meantime I triggered three more aimed rounds. The last one shattered his sternum. Driven backwards, he landed behind the other two.

I listened for movement. No telltale sounds. I took a step towards Dana to reassure her before grabbing a MAC-10, or three. That's when a high powered rifle bullet blew a shower of splinters out of the log.

Probably would have shattered my leg, if I hadn't moved.

Those three pod-brothers: bait.

I hissed at Dana to stay still. Then I bolted between some trees headed somewhat downhill. Just out of sight I jumped onto a large rock. I grabbed a tree branch with my free hand to stop. Turning, I leaped from rock to rock to hanging branch back up the hill. I let go of the branch to finish circling back to Dana.

In the next fifteen minutes I started us moving higher up the slope. As Doc's Waker pill took effect Dana began to move faster. But she started out a bit on the slender side. That meant little spare flesh for the pill to metabolize. Once that was gone her nicely toned muscles would become the drugs' target. The chemical concoction would fizzle in her a lot sooner than it would if I'd taken it.

Soon we began to double back. Because of the rock and soil composition of this side of the slope, the tree line started less than five hundred feet above us. The tree line would become a death line if we crossed it.

We stopped to give Dana a quick break. "Sir Knight," she breathed with an evil grin, "Doc knows his drugs. I have oodles and oodles of energy, but not a happy breath in the whole carload."

"Euphoric feelings are the last thing I need in my business. I'd get dead, real quick."

"Having seen a bit of your business now, I concur. But where on this flaming vertical forest are you taking me?"

"About the only place in the region I don't think they're set up to search. The other side of the ridge line. They'll be patrolling all the roads on this side. It'd be suicide to try to thumb a ride. We'd never reach a town by going through the woods.

"If we secretly top the ridge we have options. Chief Hanks place for one. There must be something important there."

"I'm almost ready to get going," said Dana, showing no sign of real fatigue. "But first, just who the flaming blazes in this Colonel? Is he a Nazi, or something? And how in Hell did he hook up with Ansie?"

"As for the two lunatics getting together... My communications expert likes to say that we're on the cusp of a new age of information and communication. This Internet thing is about to explode with useful and useless ways to spend time. The free flow of information can be the sort of thing that brings down tyrants. Or be the way that unholy individuals can get acquainted with like minded folk. I'll just bet that Anson and the Colonel found each other on some obscene Bulletin Board or Echo. They started doing some horse trading. Last I heard the Colonel worked out of Pennsylvania back country, not Colorado. Maybe Anson provided this land for the services of those crewcut pod-brothers.

"I believe the Colonel is Oliver Throckmorton. He pretends to be nearly as right-wing as Hitler. But he could care less about politics. Except as they help him out. He's a control freak. Those crewcut storm troopers are his toys. He recruits a certain type. Gets them thinking they'll one day be important to some 'New Order.' Then he makes them do whatever dirty work comes to his twisted brain. He apparently sees women only as a necessary evil. He never leaves a female survivor when he pulls up stakes. I'll bet he'd have let you 'entertain' the troops before denouncing you as a traitor. Then he'd order somebody like the trooper who blushed at frisking you to be your executioner."

Dana's eyes narrowed. She looked around, then placed her mouth in the bend of her elbow. I barely heard muttering coming from that area.

"Are you all right, Dana?"

She turned to look at me with a sheepish smile. "I had a choice. Talk literally into myself, or scream at the top of my lungs. Did I do the right thing?"

I admitted that she had as we got moving again.

We passed a hundred yards or so above the compound. Any steeper a slope Dana could not have made. I found some tripwires and dead-falls. Good ones, but they all pointed away from our line of travel. Soon the slope leveled out a bit, but trees stayed plentiful. And thank heavens they did.

I'd firmly told Dana to be quiet as possible. Meantime I dialed my hearing up as best I could. The light wind stayed from behind us. That's how I managed to hear them.

Just faint sounds. Mostly city boys trying to be quiet in the unfamiliar woods. But mixed in, almost too low to detect, came sounds of someone who knew what he was doing.

Then we reached a stretch where the going narrowed and the trees disappeared for about thirty yards. We almost sprinted across the gap. Behind a large Ponderosa pine we paused. I outlined a plan that involved taking off her blouse.

She winked at me as her fingers worked the buttons. "Why, this is so sudden…"

That sense of humor seemed nearly a divine gift. I sent her past a small grove of Aspens to another large fir of some kind. There she used small branches and twigs to fill up one shoulder of the garment.

I still had one full magazine for the Colt in reserve, and another with four rounds locked and loaded. I knew now just about how the wreck of a weapon fired. I waited, lying at the base of the Ponderosa. Dana watched for my signal.

Soon I began to see flickers of movement. The woodsman must have been directing the movements of the city boys. I'd have had trouble hitting one with a rifle, much less that Mattel quality automatic.

They paused a bit at the far edge of the gap to get organized. Then three armed pod-brothers began to move at intervals along the slope side of the gap. They'd become pretty good at using what cover there was. These tactics left a pretty clear field of fire for the rifleman.

With the first one just past the halfway point I signaled Dana. The left shoulder of the blouse eased out from behind the tree trunk as I'd instructed her. Sort of like she sought a better position. Not four seconds later came the crack of a rifle.

The pod-brothers broke cover and charged. Just like I'd hoped. My first round caught the leader right above the groin. He gave a strangled scream and pitched over into a roll. My second round zinged between the remaining two. One dived flat. The other paused, trying to find a target for the MAC-10. My third round knocked him over. I sent the fourth round at the one on the ground. To scare him, mostly. As I withdrew I heard a yelp.

I low crawled through the Aspens toward Dana's fir tree. Two rifle slugs tore over my head. The Ponderosa covered me pretty well until I reached the other forest giant. Dana had departed, per instructions.

I risked a careful look back. The first guy I'd hit apparently just kept rolling. Marks in the brush extended to the edge of a rock shelf. The second attacker seemed to be checking himself for holes as he kept flat. Then I saw his MAC-10. The thing was bent. I'd managed to hit the blessed gun. Not the gunman. Also still flat, the third one swore as he pulled a bloody hand away from his butt. Minor damage, I feared.

No sign of the woodsman with the rifle. I kept crawling. Fifty yards later I found Dana silently cursing as she tried to get the last of the brush and pine fur out of her blouse. I climbed a tree. When I had the lay of the coming land I began planning the end game.

In the meantime I surprised Dana again. Now that she had her freshly ventilated blouse back on I asked her to take off her bra. Her eyebrows shot up in surprise and with a questioning look. As we walked I used the knife to make tiny slits around the cups. At our next very brief break I laced the cups almost completely together with some of the parachute cord. Then I asked her to fill the thing up with pebbles. By then she guessed what I had in mind. Her eyes swept our path for particularly sharp bits of rock.

Only three men remained in the hunt. Two were the slightly wounded pod-brothers with a little more outdoors experience than the others. Plus the man with the long gun who acted half like a mountain man. Looking through cracks between rocks I watched them come up the first switchback.

The rifleman used hand signals to direct the other two. One of them still held a MAC-10. The other made do with a Smith & Wesson Police Positive. Dana and I lay behind two boulders up the next slope.

I'd managed, with Dana's help to wedge my wooden pry-bars where they would get the large rocks rolling with minimal effort, but not be seen.

Finally, they poked their noses around the switchback. I squeezed Dana's hand in reassurance I was not sure I really felt. I let the pod-brothers come about seven paces up the narrow slope. Now the mountain man appeared, giving them cover with his rifle.

The first of the boulders spanned nearly four feet and blocked most of the path. In a few more steps Frick and Frack would be able to see my eye at the crevice between boulder and the wall of the slope. I moved.

I lay flat along the side of the lever. On my other side sat the bra full of rocks that also now contained the small bomb Dana had smuggled out of Anson's RV. Dana lay head to head with me holding my shoulders down for dear life. Literally. I heaved on the wooden bar with all the strength I could muster. The rock tipped. A shout started from one of the pod-brothers. I kicked the thing with all my might. The sort of cylindrical boulder finally began rolling.

Now I yanked on the other lever. So hard that the much smaller rock nearly left the ground. By some minor miracle the larger boulder kept both rolling and heading down to the switchback. The smaller one hesitated for a split second before plunging over the lip to the path below.

One of the pod-brothers also dived over that lip to get away from hundreds of pounds of rolling rock. I caught just a glimpse of the rifleman ducking back around the bend.

That's when I came to my knees. Colt in one hand, I threw Dana's bra-bomb right where I thought it would do the most good.

I managed to throw myself flat just before I heard the familiar CRACK of the charge exploding. A second or so later tiny rock shards began to rain down on us.

Easing up, I looked around. I couldn't make out anybody on the down-slope. The cylindrical boulder had smashed into the wall of the switchback. Then I looked carefully over the edge. To carnage. The best I ever figured out was that the bomb bounced off the pod-brother's head as the device detonated. Not pretty. The rifleman lay bleeding out. One of the bra-cup under-wires had sliced into his jugular.

Then I heard Dana scream "Watch out!"

The next instant a bullet whistled past my ducking ear. Turned out the pod-brother with the Police Positive got lucky. The boulder had pinned him into a notch in the wall. But a slight heave and the rock rolled back, giving him a clear shot at me.

Again I threw myself to the ground. Only as I looked up did I see Dana charging the man with one of the wooden shafts. But he calmly ignored her. As I hurried to bring up the battered Colt I realized that the man's indoctrination worked against him. Women could not be warriors, the Colonel pounded that into his head. He probably figured he could handle Dana with one hand tied behind his back. Wrong on all counts, pod-brother!

I cocked the pistol as he adjusted his aim. Before I could fire Dana closed to a distance of about four feet. Without pausing the tip of the wooden shaft lashed out against the gun hand. The revolver flew towards the horizon. Now the blunt end of the wood smashed into the man's throat. Dana followed through by slamming the other end into his groin with all the force her rage could unleash. And that, as they say, was that!

On the mountain man I found a package of home jerked meat and a canteen with a few small rock holes in it. I let Dana drink what was left. She needed it much more than I did.

As we began to climb again I asked, "Dana, where in the world did you learn to do that?"

Struggling to walk, as the adrenalin rush conflicted with Doc's Waker, she replied, "I told you about Mr. Yoshida, didn't I? Anson expected me to be his sex toy. Thought every man'd love the idea. All Mr. Y. wanted was for me to treat him like a traditional submissive Japanese wife would have. And I did, most of the time.

"I'm getting tired of dodging all these flaming boulders, aren't you? Anyway, he's a student of that sword form, Kendo. Had a big exam scheduled as soon as he got back home. A main part was defending against the spear. I couldn't find a single Kendo guy in town that knew those advanced forms. Kata, I think he called them. So we went to the lumber yard and got some light poles. Then he taught me the spear forms. And an hour or two every night I went after him with a big stick. And he'd block me. If I screwed up the form too much, I'd catch his bamboo sword right where I sit down. So I learned those spear moves real well. Good thing, too.

"Oh! Before I forget it, Sir Knight. If you ask me to remove another garment, I'm going to deliberately take it the wrong way! Fair warning."

I nearly strangled on laughter as we neared the crest of the ridge.


Just over an hour later I lowered Dana from a rock ledge to behind the part of Chief Hanks' old gas station not flush with the rock wall. A moment later I joined her.

The alarms on the building had once been pretty good. And well maintained from the 1950's through about the end of the 1970's. But not since. Even without fancy tools they were fairly easy to circumvent. Soon we slipped inside.

After CPO Hanks died somebody did a good job sealing up the whole building. There was relatively little dust. And little disturbance in the office and gift shop. Only one set of footprints had explored the place in recent years. Those prints wore five-hundred dollar Italian shoes. Anson.

The garage bays were empty. The Chief's tools stood ready for an Admiral's inspection. The biggest repair bay and windowless garage door showed signs of recent use. Two trails led away from what must have been the RV's parking space. The more heavily used one ended at the metal wall covering the rock face. The second led up a flight of stairs.

To Chief Fletcher Hanks' personal quarters, as it turned out. Everything there looked just like Hanks intended to be back today. Then, in the bedroom, I found signs of things being moved.

Moved and put back. Just a little off. In the dim daylight I studied Hanks' closet.

Behind me Dana commented, "The tracks downstairs end at a solid wall. What are we doing up here?"

"What, indeed?" I replied. "The doorway seems to be downstairs. But Anson often came up here. Therefore the key to the door must be here." Less than fifteen minutes later I found it.

Never mind the details, but we heard and felt a rumbling. Back downstairs the metal wall slid back and to the side. Blinds or shutters now covered every bit of glass in the garage bays. We couldn't have seen much except for a single spotlight facing us from inside the mountain.

I kept the battered .45 in my hand. But I didn't expect to meet anyone. This was Anson's deep, dark, secret. He'd been the type not to share his toys. So we walked in.

The first room in the partially man made cave system was huge. It held several 1950's era vehicles. Plus ten very large generators. One of them roared behind a its double glass wall giving electricity to whatever the lay ahead. Off to the right we found a door leading deeper into the mountain.

We passed through a security checkpoint, but Anson had left all the safeguards inactive. Interesting, but I pressed on.

"Why didn't you take some of those guns?" asked Dana as we continued.

"The weapons are all preserved in Cosmoline. Sort of like they're coated in thick nail polish. All the ammo's at least thirty years old. Nothing I could rely on, not without a lot of testing."

"But what is this place? Fu Manchu's lair?"

"Not hardly. If old Fu owned this place we'd probably be dead by now. Let me get a look at at the chart on the wall. Then I think I can explain."

The chart turned out to be a map of the complex. And I do mean complex. I paused to absorb the thing. As I committed it to memory some bells started going off in my short term memory. I did a speed rewind of the day's adventures. A moment later I found it.

I felt Dana's hands gripping my arms as I came out of it. I smiled at her concerned look.

"Don't worry," I chuckled, "Elvis has not left the building."

"You could have warned me. I thought you might be having a cataleptic seizure. What happened."

"As I memorized the diagram this section over here came up as familiar. I had to dig pretty hard to pull of the matching memory. When we got shoved into the Colonel's office Throckmorton was covering up a diagram on the wall. That diagram matches this part of the chart."

"You don't mean that woman hater might be wandering these rooms?"

"Not a chance. Anson shared, but not anything he considered important to himself. This must be the Anson family's Cold War survival bunker. The place they could ride out the limited atomic war that a lot of people expected before there were enough nukes to wipe out the whole planet. This was set up so the whole family could live here for a long time. In the luxury they were accustomed to. Ansie decided to keep this all to himself after the family leaders abandoned it. He let Throckmorton play in this small detached section. The servants' quarters."

"That's Ansie, all right," laughed Dana. "And a hundred to one odds the Colonel thinks he's in command of all there is."

While she spoke my subconscious finished processing all the data I'd just memorized. One word at slammed into awake mind like a bucket of ice water. Dana must have thought I'd gone nuts as I grabbed her hand and nearly sprinted through the corridor's of the complex with her in tow.

Gasping for breath when we stopped, she managed to ask, "What the Hell just happened to you?"

"Serendipity," I replied. "Nothing directly to do with the mess we're in, but I've got to take a quick look. We may have just found the answer to one of the biggest mysteries of the Cold War era."

"Does that sign mean what I think it does?" said Dana, gesturing to the large heavy door in front of us. For straight ahead of us warning symbols for atomic material bracketed the single word on the door: REACTOR. When I came back out that door I think Dana checked to see if I glowed in the dim light, or had acquired a tail.

"Just enough light inside," I reported, "to tell that the atomic pile never received any fuel. Now let's get going."

"So what's the story?" asked Dana as we briskly walked through the complex.

"Ansie's great-uncle was Admiral Nelson Anson. He stayed in the Navy after World War Two. Worked closely with Hymen Rickover in the development of atomic submarines. Then, one day, in the late 1950's he wasn't in the Navy anymore. No explanation, nothing. Moved back home to live out his life with just family members for company.

"About the same time word leaked out to folks in my line of work that enough supposedly defective parts were missing to build a complete compact nuclear reactor. The story's never gone public, but more time's been expended looking for a phantom nuclear powered something-or-other than's been spent on the whole Roswell alien thing. A lot more. With zero results. Now I think we know why."

Each of the two doorways between the family and servant areas had a hidden viewport into the other area. The first one seemed to be connect to a storage area. The other showed a corridor with signs that the occupants might be packing for a quick exit. Along the way to the connections I found a fifty year old can of Three-In-One Oil. I practically emptied the thing into the machinery that opened the way into the storage area.

"Dana, I'm going to open up just enough to slip in. Close the door behind me. I'm carrying the only gizmo that will open the thing from the other side. While I'm gone see if you can find the food Anson packed in for himself. Then eat something. If I'm not back by dawn drive Anson's RV at least one hundred miles and call this number. Use the name I've written here to identify yourself. Help will be there in a big hurry. Its just a precaution. I still plan to have you marry Anson. The sooner, the better."

I think Dana almost balked at being alone again. But then she got a grip on her emotions, "Good luck, Sir Knight. I'll… I'll keep watch on the castle."

About a minute later I slipped out of the storeroom. About two minutes after that I quietly strangled the pod-brother packing up the arms room. Then, armed to the teeth, I searched the servants' quarters. I hated the killing, but all these men had pledged their loyalty to someone holding himself out as the second coming of Hitler. Or some such. Not all that many regrets.

The two silenced MAC-10's I carried kept the fight from attracting other participants. With the underground area done I headed outside.

In the small infirmary I discovered Throckmorton must have planned to start over. All the wounded were dead. Shot between the eyes with the gun pushed into the flesh. Another reason I didn't feel bad about going for a clean sweep.

I kicked in Throckmorton's office door just as he picked up a suitcase and briefcase. A Suburban with the motor running waited by the back door.

"You can't be Anson! Who are you?" he screamed as he dived for cover.

My Twilight Zone voice froze him for a split second. "I am the servant of Justice! I am Judgement." I shouted.

From behind the desk poked the snout of that fancy AK-47. By reflex I yanked out of the battered holster still on my hip the ramshackle Colt Model 1911. Before his quivering hand could fire the assault rifle I emptied the .45 into the desk. Lead and chunks of wood coming out the other side pounded the life out of Oliver Throckmorton. Before he finished dieing he managed to scramble and fall down the back stairs. I appropriated the briefcase and continued the mop-up. But he turned out to be the last one.

I stopped by Anson's RV to exchange some gear from the many hidden compartments for the briefcase. I gladly ditched the dilapidated Model 1911 for a match grade Colt Commander. Then I loaded up a Ricoh 401 single lens reflex camera and jammed extra rolls of film in my pockets.

Again in the back of the servants' quarters I worked the strange key device. Saturated with the oil I'd squirted into the mechanism, the door slid quietly back. Then came the shock.

Dana half sat, half sprawled, against the the back wall of the entryway. Visibly shaking, all of her skin not covered with makeup seemed white as a ghost.

"Dana!" I yelled as I grabbed an arm to check her pulse. Her pitiful sounding voice seemed much stronger than I expected.

"It… It's not that pill. I found… I found what Ansie was going to do with me. What he did to others. So many others…"

"Can you show me, Dana?"

"You may have to help me. I can feel Doc's Waker starting to fade. But I've got to show you what Anson did. That…"

I supported her as she pointed the way. During that trip she scorched the walls with the most lurid string of English profanity I could remember. The trip ended in the pantry.

As in the day's of the old castle keeps, the provisions were kept under the Lord's close watch. Some of the pantry's storage units still held thirty to forty year old survival rations. Anson apparently added the high cost freeze dried camping provender to a couple of shelves by the entrance. Plus some unusual tools, nicknacks, and clothing items next to the door of the huge walk-in freezer shown on the shelter map.

Dana slid out of my arms to sit on the floor, arms wrapped tightly around her knees. "In there," she said in a quivering whisper. "They're in there." She pointed to the freezer.

With camera still in hand and a sinking heart I pulled the heavy door open. One of those dangling cold storage curtains and a flurry of fog partially blocked my view. I could see a number of shapes. Human shapes. Then I pushed through to the brightly lit interior, into a chamber of horrors beyond my immediate belief.

Here lay Anson's real "art studio." Like so many young artists, his work copied the masters of old. But the Popular Park sociopath's reproductions consisted of short theater flat backgrounds and the dead frozen bodies of young women.

I retched. My head spun. I staggered to one side. My foot touched something that skidded away. When my head cleared I stood in the midst of the scene of Paul Delaroche's "The Execution of Lady Jane Gray." Only Anson depicted not the before, but the after of that event. My foot had moved the severed head a bit further from the body's neck still on the bloody block.

Some of the tableaus, older ones, I guessed, sat neatly arranged at the back of the freezer. To my right I found two unfinished ones. The first I managed to recognize without checking the attached photo of the original as Peter Paul Rubens' "Venus at the Mirror." The guy with wings holding the mirror was painted on the flat. But the slender black attendant had once been alive. Now her frozen corpse waited for Venus to arrive. Venus, no doubt, in the form of the very Rebenesque Marty. I stood there tear blinded.

When my eyes cleared again I looked at the other setting. A length of pipe rose from the back of a three foot diameter stand about a foot high. No background here. A distance mid way up the back of a seated woman the pipe branched into a sort "X" shape. Strapped to the ends of the "X" were four be-jeweled human arms. Clipped to the upright pipe was a photo of a seated statue similar to the Indian goddess Kali. The statue's body and face strongly resembled Dana when her eyes appeared Asian.

I don't know how long I stood there trying to get a grip on my emotions. Then I felt a hand on my upper arm. Dana leaned against me. She gazed up into my eyes with a haunted look. "That was for me, wasn't it?" Hesitantly she stepped forward to look at the attached picture. "This was for me," she repeated incredulously.

Cringing, Dana stepped onto the platform. She folded her legs to sit in front of the four frozen arms.

"Take my picture," she said as she brought her own arms up to match Anson's reference photo. "Take it… Please take it! I need to remember how I almost ended up. *Take my picture, dammit!!*"

One of the hardest things I ever did was to snap that shutter.

I installed Dana in the complex's high ceilinged library. Seated in a comfortable wing-backed chair, I piled some books beside her if she had the energy to try to read. I reassured her that we would leave at the earliest possible moment.

"I couldn't help you sort pennies right now," she told me. "Zero energy. Do what you have to. But please, check on me now and then."

I promised her I would, then found a secluded spot. There I called up just about every emotion controlling technique I'd ever heard of. I rose from the Lotus position nearly an unfeeling zombie.

I hurried through the bunker and out to Throckmorton's motor pool. There I made sure Anson's RV was safe to use. I pulled onto the hard-pan and wiped out the vehicle's tracks. As fast as I dared I drove the many miles to the other side of the ridge. With the RV garaged I cut back through the bunker.

I found Dana glancing through *An Anthology of Children's Literature*. When I looked in she pointed to one of the N.C. Wyeth plates. "I think I found one of your ancestors," she said with a tiny crooked smile. I thanked her as I hurried off. I'd be honored to be related to a fellow Independent Operator like Robin Hood.

Now came the hard part. I try never to think about that next hour or so. Somehow I managed to empty the few items out of the smaller freezer in the servants area. Then I crammed in Anson's gallery of horrors into the space. The final element proved too much for me. I just could not force myself to put Marty in that frozen hell. I left her sprawled just outside.

Throckmorton's second in command lay just down from the freezer door. He got off a number of rounds before I took him out. I hoped that the authorities would believe that his seeing Marty carried in started the fight that wiped out the compound.

During all of this Dana began fidgeting. I knew the feeling well. She had neither the energy to do anything, nor the ability to sleep. And would not for some time to come. I told her that only one more act remained in the "play" I was staging. Then we could leave.

Back on the other side, I put "blood" on another of the Colonel's khaki shirts. Then I did a quick and dirty job of putting his face on mine.

Beside the road I waited until I could see four cars coming on the switchback on the other side of the valley. When they approached my location I staggered to the edge of the road, brandishing the Colonel's unique red, white and blue stocked assault rifle. The cars swerved to avoid me as I fired bursts back towards the compound. Then I pretended to notice the cars. I swung the AK around, but staggered and fell. I got up before any suicidal Good Samaritan could consider stopping. Somebody in those four cars was guaranteed to call the cops.

I blocked the two concealed doors from the family area into the servants' compound. Finally I carried the drooping Dana to Anson's RV. If the cops found the whole complex, no problem. If not, the family side might be useful at some point. Not to mention the usefulness of the missing Naval Reactor 003 as leverage.

I put Dana in the RV's bed. I used extra sheets to keep her in place, but not enough to make her feel restrained should she doze off then wake up. I left the radio off as I drove towards Nevada. No need to hear what the media would make of Anson's gallery.

I spent the next day taking care of Dana. Comforting her and getting her to drink huge amounts of body builders' weight gain shake. (The stories of a major school bus tragedy in Texas and coverage of Hurricane Hugo's rampage ended up limiting the sensationalism about "Throckmorton's Gallery.") The following morning we crossed into Nevada.

If you can call any Nevada wedding chapel such, we found the most upscale one in a dozen or so counties. Then Thornton Anson, the Third, paid for flowers, a wedding dress, and sundry. Next he located the best honeymoon suite in the area. He emptied that love nest by sending the astonished occupants to Hawaii for two weeks.

That evening I carried Dana over the freshly scrubbed threshold. Soon thereafter we launched a program of recorded romantic music and shut the blinds. I slipped a couple of pieces of hardware out of our luggage. These rendered the suite door proof against anything but a battering ram.

We ate some of the fancy food and explored the facilities. Then Dana drew me into a relatively quiet corner.

"Would you please take off that mask for awhile?" she said with pleading eyes. "I don't even want to spend a false wedding night with that monster's face." When I finally complied she continued, "Your base coat of makeup has more character than Ansie ever dreamed of."

Neither of us would, or even could, touch the other's face. But the maid had a typical wedding night cleanup the following morning. I left a fifty dollar tip to help her remember.

That morning "Ansie" also mailed certified copies of the marriage paperwork to his official residence. Dana knew from his complaining that the documents would be opened, copied, and shared with the senior members of the family.

We scattered Ansie's money across Nevada for the next three days. A good amount of high cost booze went down various drains.

Then, in Searchlight, Nevada, Ansie had the RV's tank, plus the booze locker, topped off and headed for home. The following evening we met up with the small special effects and stunt team Curt Van Loan put together.

At about ten o'clock the next morning Anson's fancy recreational vehicle met a spectacular end. The forty foot beast collided with a trailer full of boiling tar. All that remained of the groom/driver was a charred skeleton. Mrs. Dana Anson miraculously survived, but with substantial facial damage due to both flying glass and burns.

Havens International Media picked up the copy from a local radio station and let the world know the details. Including the fact that, "By chance several staff members of the famous Wanamaker Clinic, on their way to a training retreat, were able to stabilize Mrs. Anson's injuries. A spokesman for the local Sheriff's Department stated that Mrs. Anson asked that her treatment be continued by the Clinic." Dana was soon airlifted east.

I'd catch up with Dana later. For now, I had to make sure all the ducks were in proper rows for the coming onslaught of investigators and lawyers that her new in-laws would even now be marshaling.

Yes, I'd catch up with Dana. In spite of my best efforts that girl got under my skin.

www.ingramcontent.com/pod-product-compliance
Lightning Source LLC
Chambersburg PA
CBHW071946170626
46813CB00005B/1840

* 9 7 8 0 6 1 5 9 9 7 4 1 4 *